RETURNABLE GIRL

Pamela Lowell

Marshall Cavendish

ACKNOWLEDGMENTS

This book is a work of fiction, but that doesn't mean it wasn't inspired. Being a family therapist gives me the honor of listening to many incredible stories. Ronnie's story was inspired by the foster and adopted children whom I've worked with through the years; however, none of the characters are real. Any resemblance to a person, living or dead, is a coincidence. Similarly, the events depicted in the book never occurred.

A novel never comes to fruition without the assistance of certain people: a special thank you to Don Judson, book coach extraordinaire, who helped shape the early stages of this manuscript; Jody Waranis and her girls' group, where we talked about cliques and what it means to be popular; Joanne Royley, who verified the authenticity of Ronnie's voice; Bri Johnson, young adult librarian, who provided teen readers and ideas on cover art; Judge Steve Lieberman, who delivered advice on legal issues and early editing; first readers Nancy Buol, Tracy Schott, Laurie Lennon, Denise Alves; my mother, Arlene Lischko, and my sisters, Jill Banister and Amy Crowley (my greatest fans); my husband, Mark, whose love and support is infinite; and my two teen sons, Edmund and Warren, for putting up with a mom who is always trying to help people and change things for the better; and finally to my agent, Susan Schulman; and editors at Marshall Cavendish, especially Margery Cuyler and Marilyn Mark, who recognized that Ronnie deserved a home.
—P.L.

Marshall Cavendish Corporation
99 White Plains Road
Tarrytown, NY 10591
www.marshallcavendish.us

Library of Congress Cataloging-in-Publication Data
Lowell, Pamela.
Returnable girl / by Pamela A. Lowell.
p. cm.
Summary: Friendship with an outcast classmate and memories of her mother's desertion interfere with the relationship thirteen-year-old Ronnie tries to establish with her new foster mother.
ISBN-13: 978-0-7614-5317-8
ISBN-10: 0-7614-5317-2
[1. Foster home care—Fiction. 2. Mothers—Fiction. 3. Friendship—Fiction.] I. Title.
PZ7.L9646Re 2006
[Fic]—dc22
2006006398

The text of this book is set in Transitional 511.
Book design by Anahid Hamparian

Printed in China
First edition
10 9 8 7 6 5 4 3 2 1
mc Marshall Cavendish

For foster girls and
boys everywhere

Part One
Abandoned

This is the first time I remember my mother leaving me.

It is dark out. Snow is falling. My nose is pressed against the bedroom window. I am watching my mother shovel snow off her car.

She turns, blows me a kiss, and then motions for me to get into bed.

It seems to take forever for her to come back inside.

Finally she opens my bedroom door. "I was putting the baby to sleep," she says.

"And getting ready to go out, right?"

She has black-lined eyes and blue-red lips. Out loud I count five tiny silver hoops in her ear. She's wearing stockings. A short dress. High heels.

"You look pretty."

"You think?" she replies, smiling coyly.

Snuggling up beside me on the bed, she reads me a story. So close, I can smell the mouthwash on her breath. (Only later I learned it was to cover up the alcohol.) She checks her watch. Suddenly, she shuts the book and tosses it on the floor.

"I gotta go, Veronica."

"One more story. One more!"

"No!" she yells. Then she smiles and touches my hair. "I can't be late." She stands up and starts for the door.

"But Uncle Melvin and Raylene said I have to say my prayers!"

My uncle and Raylene are away on a church trip, which is why they can't watch me tonight. I get down off my bed and kneel on the floor. The floor is carpeted with thin, scratchy fuzz. It's hard, and my knees hurt, but I'll do anything to get her to stay.

"Now I lay me down to sleep," I begin.

"Can't you say them after I go?"

"Almost done. If. I. Should. Die. Before. I. Wake." I stretch out my words, making my prayers especially slow while trying to think up something else to tell her.

"Raylene says 'my soul to keep' means Jesus is my personal savior."

"Whatever." Mom picks at one of her nails. Her nails are painted black. Raylene would say they were black as sin.

"See? There he is." I point at the statue of Jesus that Raylene bought me for being saved. Jesus's face looks kind of like my uncle's—if I squint really hard.

"Does he still watch over me when you're not here?"

"What?" she snaps. "Who are you talking about?"

"Jesus."

"Shit. I don't know. Why don't you ask him?"

"You really think he'll answer me?"

The plastic Jesus statue sits on my dresser next to the night-light. His beady eyes seem to pierce right through me, and real-looking blood leaks down his chest. Sometimes I call him the Scary Jesus, but never in front of any grown-ups.

"Look, Ronnie, I don't have time for—"

"But what if I die before I wake?"

"You won't," she says, pulling back the covers. I'm still kneeling on the floor. "Hurry up! Get in! Kenny gets real mad if I make him wait."

"Mommy. Stay with me. Please." I grab at her neck before she's out of reach.

"Stop it!" She wrenches herself away. "You can do this for me, Veronica. Don't be such a baby." She's standing at my door.

"I'm not! You're mean. I hate you!"

"But I'll always love you," she says, blue-red lips set in a line. "Home soon, I promise. Remember, Mrs. Holiday's next door if you need her." She closes my door partway.

The room is dark.

Monsters-under-the-bed dark.

Except for the milky-white glow from the hallway and the streetlight reflecting on the snow.

I lie in bed and try to keep my eyes fixed on the night-light, but they keep darting over to the statue of Jesus. I can't stop staring at the blood dripping down his chest, and I imagine it's dripping across the top of my dresser. Drip, drip, drip—all the way down to the floor. I make sure I'm positioned carefully, in the middle of my big-girl bed. Not a foot or a hand hanging over the side.

My ears are wide open. First, I hear my mother scraping the ice from the windshield of her car; then the sound of the engine as she drives away; and then the quiet of my breathing, and the TV from Mrs. Holiday's apartment through the wall.

No baby crying. Not yet.

Click. Click. Click.

What's that noise?

The clicking of hail on the windows sounds like someone trying to get in.

Don't worry. I'll keep you safe. No one is trying to get in.

That's what Jesus seems to tell me, but his lips don't move. I'm praying my mother will come back soon.

What if the baby cries?

"You'll hear him," my mother told me. "Give him a bottle. Tilt it up for him, okay?"

But my brother doesn't wake.

I watch the digital clock on my night-stand.

But what if Mrs. Holiday won't answer her door?

"Call me. Just press number one. But only if it's an emergency."

Is staying awake all night long an emergency?

I must have fallen asleep because the next thing I remember is my mother's knees pressing into my back as she crawls into bed with me, somewhere near dawn. "G'night," she mumbles, slurring her words.

I arrange the covers around her and then I pet her long black hair.

That wasn't so bad, I remember thinking. She was right. I could do this whenever she needed me to. I was almost six years old.

September 12

Veronica Hartman has been returned nine times between the ages of eleven and thirteen.

That's what it says in my file, but if you include the return by my uncle and Raylene the week before Christmas almost two years ago, then it really has been a total of ten times—so far. The last time, I got kicked out of Lancaster Academy for throwing a pair of scissors at my art teacher. And the time before, I buried my foster mother's keys in the backyard behind the barn. That number doesn't include the times I had to stay at the shelter, or the overnight emergency placements; I can't even remember most of those.

"All that returning can do some damage," Alison says, "but you've got to find ways to cope."

Alison Hauser is my foster mom (at the moment) and she's also a therapist. She hasn't returned me yet, and I've been with her over three months, but that doesn't mean she won't. Lately, I guess, she's been considering it. Like this morning, for instance, after I threw the can of frozen orange juice across the kitchen.

"I'm not a thief!" I screamed at her as I let the can fly.

"Shit!" said Alison, ducking out of the way. "Then, where's the money, Ronnie? It was here last night." She picked up the can, which had landed on the floor next to the sink. "This could have seriously injured me. I thought we were well past all that! What did I say would happen if you ever threw something at me again?"

It didn't surprise me in the least that she would threaten to send me back; eventually, it seems, they all do. Even Alison, with her long, graying hair and her plump stomach that looks soft and cushiony like a broken-in sofa you might want to curl up on someday.

"Oh, please," I said calmly. "I didn't throw it *at* you, and it missed you by a mile. You know I don't like to be accused of things—it's in my file. But if you can't handle it, I'll go upstairs and get my bag—it's ready, like always. Just say the word and I'm sure Midge will come get me."

I was thinking about the black Hefty bag where I keep all of my worldly possessions, still unpacked in the corner of my room, and Midge, my caseworker, who transports me from place to place.

Walking over to the stairs, I stuffed what was left of a cold English muffin into my mouth. "Oh, and one more thing," I added, licking the crumbs off my fingers. "Should you really be cursing? Aren't you supposed to be setting an example?"

I tapped my foot on the floor. "Well? Do you want me to get my bag or not?"

Alison shook her head and sighed. "Look, Ronnie, either hand over the cash or I'm calling Midge. I mean it! I'm getting tired of this. I don't have time to stop at the bank this morning, and you need to get to school."

She picked up the phone. "I'm dialing."

I didn't really believe that Alison wanted to send me back—not yet, anyway. She's a *psychologist*, an expert on "problem" kids. That's why I was sent to her in the first place—no other foster homes would take me. But if I didn't want to be locked up in some prisonlike treatment center, I figured I'd better, as Midge says, "Get with the program."

Turning on my heel, I walked into the living room. "Oh. Hey. What the heck is this?" I called in a voice as nice as could be. "Alison? Could you come in here a sec?"

Alison stopped dialing and followed me into the room. Her new black-heeled loafers made an I-mean-business-sounding noise on the hardwood floor. She was wearing her work clothes: a white cable-knit sweater over a long, denim skirt. "Approachable" clothes, she calls them, so her patients feel safe.

I was sitting on one of her two faded paisley love seats, holding a small, cloth-covered Bible in my hand. (I still believe in God, even after all that's happened to me.)

"Is this what you've been looking for?" I asked, trying to sound innocent. Stuck like a bookmark between two pages was the twenty-dollar bill.

"I suppose now you're going to tell me that *God* put it there," she said.

I could tell she meant it sarcastically.

"Maybe God *wanted* me to put it there," I answered, trying to come up with a quick excuse. "Maybe he was hoping you'd look for it after I left for school, and then you'd find it and sit down and read a few verses . . . or something." I shrugged.

Even I was having trouble buying this one.

Alison's eyebrows knitted together, making creases on her forehead. She brushed a stray hair from her face. "Can we please get honest here? You stole something from me and now you're lying about it, and blaming *God*, for goodness' sake."

She was right about the stealing. Why had it seemed like such a good idea last night? But she was wrong about God. (I happen to know a lot of people who blame God when things go wrong; Raylene used to do it all the time.)

I got up from the love seat, pulled my backpack over

my shoulder, and stomped toward the door.

Alison walked across the room and slipped the money from out of the Bible into her purse, grabbed her keys and briefcase from the dining-room table, and turned on the dishwasher in the kitchen. We were just about ready to leave when I opened the refrigerator door. "Where's my lunch?" I asked.

Her face crumpled. "Damn! With all that commotion, I forgot to pack it. And now I don't have time."

She quickly looked in her wallet for some singles (no luck), then dumped her whole purse out on the countertop, hoping for some spare change (which she didn't find either). So, guess what? She had to hand over the same twenty-dollar bill that she'd accused me of stealing about five minutes earlier.

"Here," Alison said grumpily.

It was hard not to laugh, but I managed.

"Try not to look so triumphant, okay? I'm expecting some change," she said, as if I was the kind of person who would keep it.

"You really don't know me at all," I said coldly.

I shot her a dirty look, and tears sprang to her eyes. I hadn't expected that. She looked so defeated that I decided to give her a small hug before I left.

Alison pulled me close, her gold charm bracelet tinkling in my ear. "I could if you'd let me," she whispered.

Then she locked the door behind us. I walked quickly down the alleyway toward the bus stop, trying not to be late and wondering whether I'd remembered to do all my homework, when Alison suddenly called to me from her car. "Wait! Ronnie!"

What did she want *now*?

I turned around, annoyed.

"No using the computer today!" she yelled. "We can work on the stealing, but I don't want you throwing things. You need to start thinking before you act. No more violence or you're going back. I mean it!"

September 20

Midge draws her eyebrows in high, rust-colored arches, giving her a constantly surprised-looking expression. She said that it might be a good idea for me to start writing things down on account of how much I've been bounced from place to place. She went to this conference in Kutztown where they told her that kids transitioning from foster care don't have anyone to "reminisce" with about their life stories.

"Trust me," she said in her raspy smoker's voice as she handed me a disk. "Someday you'll want to remember everything that's happened to you."

Not *everything*, I wanted to tell her.

Midge likes to think this is her best idea ever, but I would have written stuff down anyway because I love to write. I plan to write a novel about my life and adventures that will probably get made into a movie someday starring a girl who has long wispy hair (parted in the middle), smudgy green eyes, and a half-decent smile (with braces). This actress will also be very smart and love dogs.

Usually I keep the disk in my Hefty bag, the one I packed the day my mother left me—it's safe there— except last weekend I was downloading some music onto this new computer that Alison bought me and I accidentally deleted *everything*!

My entire life story!

I had to start all over again!

AGGHHH!

Alison gave me a separate disk for my music and said from now on I should just save my story on the hard drive. She also told me not to be so upset, that writing my story again might give me a different perspective.

I'm guessing Alison has never been deleted.

Now, why I don't like Midge:

"So what bothers you most about being abandoned?" Midge asked me once, without any feeling at all, like, *what bothers you most about getting a C on your math test?*

Most? Well, for starters, it bothers me that I can't remember what my mother looks like, that I have to take her photograph out of my bag and trace the creases with my finger so they lie flat. It's the only picture I have of her and my brothers, taken in front of the restaurant in Alaska where she worked when they first left me. There's a lot of snow there, more snow than I've ever seen before, and it's in piles as high as her shoulders. The sign out front says ARCTIC TACOS.

It's hard for me to imagine eating hot, spicy tacos in freezing-cold Alaska. Actually, it's hard for me to imagine doing *anything* in Alaska since I've never been there and Mom's still not ready for me—yet.

Midge said she thought it was especially cruel that my mother would send me a picture with Derek and Danny standing right next to her, looking so cute in their light blue parkas, while I'm stuck here without a mom. I didn't mind, though; I mean, they are my half brothers. They used to call me Sis. Mom knew I'd want to see how big they'd grown since I'd seen them. It was mostly me who had taken care of them when she and her boyfriend Kenny were out working, or socializing, or whatever it was they did all the time when they weren't home. We never found out who Derek's dad was, but Kenny (who I **hate**, obviously) was/is Danny's father. My mother isn't living with him anymore, which is a good thing, because he is truly evil. But all the same, because of Midge's comment about the picture, I don't show it to therapists or caseworkers or any of those do-gooders anymore. Besides, another reason I don't like Midge is that she keeps telling me that my mom might not *ever* be ready for me—so why would I want to share anything with her?

Actually, when I talked to my mom on the phone last month she told me about her new waitress job. But she also said, "My car keeps breaking down. You gotta be patient. It costs more to live here than in Pennsylvania. I'm trying to save money so I can bring you up here— *soon.*"

I want to believe her, but Midge told me she's been failing her drug screens again. Mom admitted to me that her new boyfriend has a "slight" problem with smoking pot, and that sometimes she "relaxes" with him too. She emphasized the word *slight* when we talked last month, but I took it to mean much more. Like what if she's going with another druggie loser?

Somebody like Kenny?

Smoking marijuana always leads her to drinking and doing other drugs. How many more times am I supposed to go through this?

But even if my mother *was* ready to bring me up there, Midge probably wouldn't let me go. Not for a while, anyway. At least not until Alison helps me with my "impulsive behavior" and "abandonment issues."

That's all I want to write about for now, because when I start thinking about my mother and my little brothers, I get really depressed and it always leads me back to thinking about the day she left with Kenny, which was the **worst day of my whole entire life** and I'm positive I don't want to *ever* think about that day again.

September 29

You won't believe what happened this morning after I got to the bus stop, which is right at the end of our block. Mostly it seemed the same as any other morning since I started going to Liberty Middle School last June, except that now it's late September and I'm in eighth grade and the oak trees are golden and there are tons of acorns all over this street.

(I love the word *golden*. Besides *caprice*, it's my absolutely **favorite** word.)

Paige was there, with Sarika and Britnee and a couple of other kids—but not Cat, who is my only friend and who sometimes gets migraines on Mondays.

First I want to describe Paige, since practically every girl in this school wishes she were Paige Jamison. Paige is so popular and really, really thin. Even her eyebrows are shaped especially thin and pointy, like a model's. She has long, chestnut-brown hair that she is constantly rearranging, and when she walks it swings back and forth between her shoulders like a separate body part.

Her eyes are her best feature (when they aren't judging you). They are wide-set apart and almost turquoise, with thick, long fringy lashes. Today she wore a tight lavender tube top and low-rise jeans. On her feet were matching lavender sandals (with a wedge).

Sarika had her dark hair pulled back in a puffy ponytail, and the diamond stud in her nose sparkled like a tiny star.

Britnee's shoulder-length hair was still wet from her shower. Her hair looks brown when wet, but it's actually golden, like the color of a bale of hay. She was combing it with her fingers, and shaking it back and forth to dry.

It was warm out, but the three of them were wearing white Windbreakers with red letters that said, "Liberty Elite Girls Soccer." I don't play soccer. I want to, but I've never stayed in one place long enough to be any good.

Britnee and Sarika are always with Paige, I mean *constantly* because they are the three most popular girls at school. Sometimes it's like they are one person instead of three. I stood off near the curb, hoping that they wouldn't notice me—or maybe hoping that they *would*, but in a nice way for a change.

Sure enough, in a few minutes, Paige wobbled over to me in her too-high lavender sandals. "You're wearing that stupid shirt again?" she said, her turquoise eyes piercing mine. "You wore it like three times last week."

I gave her a look like, *and your point is?*

I hadn't realized anyone was keeping track. Of course she wouldn't know that wearing this shirt makes me feel close to my mother, who sent it to me for my birthday last year. It has a picture of Mount McKinley on it and the words, "The Great One." I don't care if it's oversized, stained, and faded—it's one of my favorites.

Paige stared at me intently. "You could be almost

pretty if you tried a little harder. Don't you get a clothing allowance from the state?"

I wanted to punch her extremely hard when she said that. My eyes welled up and my hand clenched into an automatic fist, but then I remembered what Alison had said about no more violence.

"Look, I have plenty of damn clothes, okay?"

This was true. Alison had bought me a bunch of new outfits when I first moved here. There were more clothes in my closet than I'd ever had before.

"Don't get so defensive," said Paige. "I was only trying to help."

Was she serious?

"Maybe somebody doesn't want our help," said Britnee, looking down at her French-manicured fingernails.

"Didn't we stop wearing shirts like that in third grade?" asked Sarika. Her teeth were small and white against her coffee-colored skin.

I was trying very hard not to cry.

Paige must have noticed my expression because she arched one of her thin eyebrows and flicked her perfect, shiny hair. "What's wrong?" she said. "Can't you take a little constructive criticism?"

I took a deep breath. "Sure I can. Thanks for the tip."

I tried to smile to show that I was one of them, but I'm *not* one of them—although I'd really like to be. More than anything! They all wear cropped shirts and designer *everything* and live in big, beautiful houses with perfect families. Their lives are *perfect*. And mine is not. But neither is Cat's, who as I said is my only friend and wasn't there because she sometimes gets migraines on Mondays.

Now I need to tell you about Cat. Weird, funny, crazy, chubby Cat.

Cat's not hugely overweight, but she's very round and "big-boned" enough for everything to look too tight on her, and she's overly developed, if you know what I mean. She dyes her choppy-cut, chin-length hair pitch-black and wears mostly all-black clothes, so she's sort of Goth—but in a sweet kind of way.

Cat came up to me my very first morning at the bus stop last June, when there was barely a month left to go of seventh grade.

"Hey, you're new here, right?" Cat said, chewing on a fingernail. She'd caught me staring at Paige who was standing in a circle with the other pretty girls. I remember feeling awkward and wanting to join them—but they weren't exactly making any efforts to approach me.

Cat motioned me closer. "Paige is the bitch of our school," she said, as if reading my mind. "You don't want to be friends with her." I looked at Cat with her weird clothes and her choppy hair, and I remember thinking, okay, but why should I be friends with you?

We all got on the bus for the ten-minute ride to school. I stared out the window, pretending to be interested in the scenery, while a pimply-faced boy wearing over-sized headphones sat next to me.

During that first day's morning classes, I tried to size up who was nice, who was smart, who to watch out for, and where I could fit in. But by lunchtime, I still didn't know who I was going to eat with (no one had asked me).

Cat spied me standing anxiously at the front of the cafeteria with my tray and motioned me over to her table. It felt so good to have somebody notice me that I didn't care anymore what she looked like—or the fact that no one else was sitting at her table.

When we got off the bus together at the end of the day, I watched as Paige and her friends headed the opposite way, without so much as a glance in our direction. Cat surprised me by asking if I wanted to hang out for a while. "Come on," she said, following my gaze. "We'll go for a tour. I'll show you where the rich kids live."

It was muggy and the air felt heavy, like there might be a thunderstorm later. We walked the two short blocks to her house. Cat's house was the same style as Alison's: a raised ranch. Except that Alison's place was neat and tidy, with flowering window boxes and the sidewalk swept clean. Cat's house was obviously in need of painting, two gray shutters were hanging loose, and the grass was so long it was almost going to seed. It was one of the few rental houses in Liberty, Cat told me, and her mother complained to their landlord all the time, but he just didn't seem to care.

"So did your dad get transferred?" she asked when we got inside. She handed me a Diet Coke from the fridge and took one for herself.

"Huh?" I said.

"Why else would you move here at the end of the school year?"

What was I supposed to tell her? That this was my tenth foster home? My very last chance?

"I don't really have a dad," I explained. "My mom lives in Alaska. I'm in foster care."

"Oh. Sorry," she said, looking surprised. "You don't act like a foster kid. But I only knew one." A smile lit up her eyes. "He used to wet his pants every day in second grade."

"Thanks," I said, laughing. "I think."

She smiled again and then she looked curious. "Is it

really that bad?" she said. "Being on your own, I mean. Without anyone telling you what to do?"

I almost made up a story about how cool it was, but then, I guess because she didn't seem to be judging me, the truth rushed out instead.

"It totally sucks," I replied.

Cat nodded like she understood. "If it makes you feel any better, I don't live with my dad either. Just my mom and older brother. And my mother's asshole boyfriend, Bud."

I smiled when she said that, realizing maybe she didn't have it so great either.

When we finished our sodas, we went outside and walked the five blocks toward the boulevard and then we took a left. Penn Avenue has a median of trees right down the middle, dividing both sides of the street. The houses there are enormous—like mansions! They are made of brick or stone with three-story additions, a Mercedes in every driveway, and tennis courts swallowing up their side yards. It was like a different world existed only five blocks away!

"That's where Paige lives," Cat told me, pointing across the street. "Her father's a doctor."

I gazed at the huge yellow Victorian with green shutters and cut-out trim. It reminded me of a fancy gingerbread house you might see decorated in the stores at Christmastime—only giant-sized, perfectly landscaped, with fountains and everything!

"That's got to be the most beautiful house I've ever seen!"

Cat shrugged. "Paige's mother won't even say hello to my mom in the grocery store. Her whole family is stuck-up like that."

"Nice," I said sarcastically, but that didn't stop me

from wishing I could live in a house like that someday.

Cat kicked at a rock with her shoe. "Sometimes I sneak out at night and knock over their trash cans so their garbage spills into the street."

That surprised me. "And you do that *because* . . . ?"

"I don't know," she said. "Just to mess with them, I guess."

I looked at her sideways. A new picture of her was starting to form in my mind, like maybe we had a lot in common after all.

Once school let out for the summer, Cat came over to Alison's house to get me almost every day. Sometimes we hung out at Cat's house and watched TV, but mostly we just swam in her pool—except when Alison had some lame chore for me to do like vacuum the whole entire house.

We were fast becoming good friends. ☺

I confided in Cat about wanting to write about my life's adventures in a novel one day, and she showed me her notebook filled with poems. (Most of them were pretty depressing, but I told her they were great.)

One lazy afternoon in mid-July, it was so hot out that you couldn't walk barefoot in the street. We were floating on tubes in Cat's small, aboveground pool, holding glasses of diet iced tea in our hands. Cat was practically falling out of her bathing suit—a low-cut, black tankini. I noticed she hadn't lost any weight over the summer yet, like she'd planned.

"Oh. My. God!" she said, quickly crossing her arms in front of her.

"What?"

"Up at the window. It's Bud. He's spying on us!"

I screamed. "Gross!"

I watched him pull down the shade, but my shriek-
ing had made her dog, King, start running in circles
around the pool. Cat was yelling at him to stop barking
when all of a sudden we saw Paige and Britnee walking
down the street. They were wearing identical white
skirts and carrying tennis rackets and water bottles.

"Oh, great," said Cat in a way that meant just the
opposite.

Of course, they noticed us right away because Cat's
pool has a rusty wire fence around it and it sits in full
view of the curb.

"Hey, Cat!" called Britnee loudly. "Somebody tried
to sign you up for swim team today. At the country
club."

"What?" Cat slipped out of her tube, as if she knew
that couldn't be true.

"Yeah," said Paige, laughing. "But we told her not
to—'cause you'd definitely sink."

Cat's cheeks burned red as she turned away from
them.

I didn't think that was very funny. I was feeling
really sorry for Cat, but when I glanced over at her, her
lips curved into a strange little smile.

"Watch this, Ronnie," she said quietly. She lowered
herself into the shallow water. Then she crossed her
arms in front of her, grabbed at the edge of her tankini,
and whipped off the top of her bathing suit!

She *flashed* them!

Her huge white breasts looked even whiter against
her tan.

" I will never forget the look of shock on Paige's and
Britnee's faces. "Oh my God! That's *disgusting*!" they
screamed.

As we watched them run down the block, Cat and I laughed so hard our stomachs hurt. "I thought that might get rid of them," Cat said smugly, pulling the straps back over her shoulders. "I just hope Bud wasn't watching."

That got us laughing even harder.

I admired her nerve. "Where'd you get the guts to do that?"

She thought for a minute. "I'm not sure. Something about you being here, Ronnie. It must've made me feel less afraid."

And that's how it was between us.

When the bus came around the corner this morning after Paige had made fun of my shirt, I climbed on, and the rest of Monday went on, business as usual, with people mostly ignoring me. I ate lunch all by myself (because Cat wasn't there), and as always, daydreamed about the day when my mother would finally take me out of this place and bring me to live with her and my brothers in Alaska.

Oh, except for one other thing. When I was hurrying to get onto the bus, I made sure to stand right behind Paige. It was tricky because Britnee tried to squeeze me out, but somehow I managed to hold my ground. I had a black Magic Marker with me, a permanent black ink one (like the one Alison uses to address packages), which had somehow made its way into my pocket.

Now, I'm not exactly sure how this next part happened, but as we were climbing up the bus stairs, I uncapped the marker and "accidentally," really quickly, secretly, sort of scribbled onto the back of Paige's white Liberty Elite Soccer Windbreaker.

The letter *B*. (For *bitch*.)

Then I worried the whole rest of the day that she would discover it was me.

October 11

It wasn't my fault I got strep throat! You'd think I did it on purpose the way Alison went around unpacking, slamming drawers, and acting all huffy, just because she was going to miss out on her once-a-year "self-care" weekend with her girlfriends, who all happen to be therapists just like her.

I do feel sort of bad about Alison not going, though. She works awfully hard with those crazy patients of hers, and she does drag me around to my appointments, so she really could use a break, which is why foster kids get put into "respite" in the first place.

RESPITE SUCKS. That's what I carved into my dresser upstairs when she told me three days ago that I had to go, but now I don't, and I'm glad, glad, *glad*!

I mean, how would you like to stay with a strange family that you don't know *at all*, for an *entire* weekend and pretend that you're having a good time? Wouldn't you mind them watching you extra careful because they've heard about your "problems" and have probably had access to your "file," which by the way, is *wicked* thick—like two files, or maybe three or four?

Getting sick was worth it—almost. Now I'm upstairs in my room under the covers in my cozy bed, looking at the pictures of different dogs I'd like for a pet someday. I've taped them on the wall above my desk. My black plastic bag is tucked in the corner of my room, under a pile of clothes that never seem to get put away. Alison is taking really good care of me today. After she found out I wasn't faking it like she suspected, that I actually had *strep throat*, her "affect" completely changed and she got all nice and sympathetic.

(*Affect* is how therapists talk about moods. Once I overheard Alison talking on the phone to Midge about my affect, which is usually, I'll admit, pretty bad. For example, when I first got here and my mother didn't show up for our monthly phone call, I came back from Midge's office and punched a hole in the wall above my bed; but Alison made me fix it using Spackle and some paint.)

"Are you feeling any better?" Alison asked, bringing in some homemade chicken soup with dumplings for lunch and Jell-O—just like a real mother would. Alison is a great cook, by the way, because she's Pennsylvania Dutch. But that doesn't mean she's Dutch at all; she explained to me that her ancestors were from Germany.

"You're looking a little pale," she added.

"My throat still hurts pretty bad." I found it very hard to swallow, like sharp razor blades were cutting into my tonsils. I tried to sniff at the rose she'd put in the vase on the wooden tray, but I couldn't smell a thing.

Pushing a strand of hair behind my ear, Alison felt my forehead. "You're still warm," she said. Her charm bracelet glittered in the sunlight. She took a thermometer from her sweater pocket and stuck it in my mouth, just as the phone downstairs began to ring.

"Leave it there till I get back." She picked up some tissues from the floor, and closed the squeaky door gently behind her.

While Alison was gone I started thinking about yesterday, which was almost a complete disaster, but also one of the BEST days of my entire life.

It all began at the bus stop. Paige was showing off this beautiful new necklace she had gotten for her birthday. It was a chunky Tiffany heart choker, all bright sterling silver, and she told us that it cost over two hundred dollars. Paige said that she would let us all feel how heavy it was, "but only my *real* friends can try it on." Then she smiled at me, only I couldn't tell whether it was a nice smile or not.

Cat was sitting on the curb reading the latest Harry Potter book, in her jeans and a baggy sweatshirt. She looked up at me through frizzy black bangs when Paige said that, like, *does she dream up ways to torture us in her sleep?*

Sarika and Britnee went immediately to the front of the line. I thought the idea was kind of lame, but since everyone else was doing it and I *really* liked that necklace, I got in line with them to see which one of us would get a turn. I let Cat cut in front of me.

Of course, Paige let every single girl who was there try it on, but when it came to be Cat's turn (right before mine), she gave Cat a nasty look and immediately refastened the necklace. "What are you *thinking*?" she said cruelly, tossing her long brown hair. Then she looked at me and kinda shrugged.

Then everybody at the bus stop laughed and got into a circle that shut us out. I felt like the biggest fool. I was thinking, what if I hadn't let Cat get in front of me? Would I have had a turn? But I pushed those thoughts out of my mind.

As Cat sidled up to me, I whispered, "I guess we were *thinking* that for once in her life she wouldn't be such a mean little *bitch*."

Cat, of course, thought that was *too* funny. She

laughed her loud, crazy laugh. "I'm so happy you moved here," she said, standing overly close to me as usual.

I suddenly wished that her laugh wasn't so loud . . . or so crazy. I stepped away. "Me, too," I replied, but I wasn't sure whether I was happy or not.

Still, I couldn't stop thinking about that necklace all the way to school, and apparently neither could Cat. In science, second period, she wrote me a note. The note said that her brother knew how to order fake Tiffany necklaces over the Internet, and wouldn't it be fun if we could somehow switch Paige's real necklace with a fake one?

Paige is such a <u>bitch</u>, Cat wrote. *She deserves it.* And then she signed her name like she always does by drawing a picture of a cat in the circle of the letter *a*.

One thing about Cat, she sure could come up with some wild schemes to get back at Paige, but she couldn't seem to tell her off face-to-face.

Cat gets made fun of by just about everybody at school and it must get to her pretty bad. Sometimes after they tease her I swear there's a deep, sad emptiness in her almost-black eyes, right where her happiness is supposed to be. I put the note from her into my pocket but I couldn't stop thinking about that necklace.

Pretty soon it was lunchtime. When we were finished eating, I went over to Sarika who was standing near where we dump our trays.

"Why wouldn't Paige let me try on her necklace?" I asked, hoping Sarika might be honest since the others weren't there.

She looked sort of surprised that I would ask.

I cleared my tray into the garbage can. "I mean,

does Paige really hate me . . . or is it something else?"

Sarika narrowed her almond-shaped eyes, and shook her head. "Oh, Ronnie, she doesn't hate *you* at all. Paige thinks you're pretty. It's just that everyone knows Cat is so *weird*, and you kinda hang out with her."

The diamond stud in her nose twinkled at me.

I suddenly realized that what Sarika told me was unbelievably important. She was trying to do me a favor. If I wanted to fit in, I needed to pay attention.

It was just as I'd suspected! But could it really be that simple?

Could Cat be the only thing standing between me and being popular?

I needed time to think. Paige, Britnee, and Sarika all had gym class next, with Cat and me, in the musty-smelling basement of the school. As I walked down the staircase behind Paige, I traced my fingers along the grout-lines of the mint green tile and wondered what I should do.

We changed into our gym clothes and then divided up into six teams because we were playing volleyball. When it was my turn to serve, I pretended that I had just gotten my period. I told Miss Riley, our gym teacher (who has knobby knees), that I had cramps and needed to go to the nurse, but I went into the girls' locker room instead. First I went into the bathroom to check and see if I really did get it because I had been sort of emotional lately (according to Alison), but I hadn't.

I thought about going back into the gym because our team was winning and it was fun to be winning for a change, but something stopped me. I walked from the bathroom into the locker room again, until I was standing right next to Paige's gym locker. I stood there for what seemed like five whole minutes . . . at least.

My heart started beating really fast and I felt a trickle of sweat gather and run down under my arm, like it always does when I'm about to do something wrong. Before I knew it, I had rifled through Paige's clothes and found her necklace on the top shelf of her locker, which is, coincidentally, the locker right next to mine.

It was almost too easy.

The lockers aren't ever locked. We don't lock them since they are so old—like from the sixties—and they are constantly jamming and getting stuck.

Paige's necklace was icy cold and heavy like it was made of pure silver. The heart charm was perfectly shaped, and it had the word "Tiffany" engraved right on it. When I poured the chain from hand to hand it made a gentle, clinking sound. It was so beautiful I almost cried. I ran over to the mirror and put it on.

I have to say it looked pretty great.

Then I took the necklace and put it into *Cat's* locker— in one of her shoes. Don't ask me why I did this. At first I thought that I was doing something nice for Cat because it was obvious that she really wanted that necklace, too, but thinking back on it, maybe that wasn't the real reason after all. Somehow everything got all twisted around in my head and later it turned into something else completely.

After gym, when we were getting changed out of our gym clothes and sneakers, Paige noticed right away that her necklace was missing. "I can't find my *necklace!*" she shouted.

"Maybe it fell off when you were serving?" I offered, sneaking a glance at Cat.

"I'm not stupid," Paige said. "I know I took it off before gym."

"Sometimes I forget where I put things," said Cat, untying her sneaker. "Then I find them the next day."

"Shut up," said Britnee. "You don't have *anything* that nice."

Paige began to yell. "It's been *stolen*! Somebody stole my new necklace!"

"Ronnie, weren't you talking to me about it at lunchtime?" asked Sarika curiously.

"Give me a break," I replied, my heart beating fast.

Miss Riley came running into the locker room after hearing Paige's screams, and I noticed Cat's black eyes get really wide. She looked at me like, *did you do anything?*

I rolled my eyes, like Paige was being a drama queen, as usual.

Then Miss Riley went around slamming our lockers shut and said none of us were going anywhere until this was resolved. "I don't care if you're late for class."

The gym office smelled funky, like the rest of the gym: a mixture of old sneaker smell and BO. Miss Riley took us back there one by one. Britnee was first, then Sarika, then me. I don't know what she said to them, but when it was my turn, she said, "You had some problems at your old school, didn't you, Ronnie?"

I shrugged.

Her fingers went to the whistle around her neck. "You left class for a few minutes to go to the nurse. Did you make any detours along the way?"

It was almost as if she could read my mind. She was looking at me so suspiciously that I had to think really fast. How had it suddenly come down to this? This was getting serious, I realized. It was going to be either me getting into serious trouble—or *Cat.*

Even though the Christian part of me wanted to, I just couldn't tell Miss Riley the truth. I couldn't risk being kicked out of another school again! This was my last chance. So I didn't lie, but I didn't exactly tell the whole truth, either.

"Well, Miss Riley, Cat *was* saying that she liked that necklace when everybody was trying it on this morning at the bus stop. Now, I don't want to get anybody in trouble or anything . . . but she *did* give me this note in science class."

I pulled Cat's note from my pocket and handed it to her.

Miss Riley scanned the note quickly. "I'm sure this will be very helpful. It's not easy telling on a friend. Thanks for being so honest."

Honest? I was going straight to hell.

Of course when Miss Riley went back into the locker room and marched directly to our row of lockers and opened Cat's locker, the necklace was there, right in Cat's shoe where I left it.

It got really quiet. Everyone began whispering. *Sure, who else? We all knew it just had to be Cat.*

Cat's eyes brimmed over with tears. She looked over at me, speechless.

Afterward, it quickly got around the whole school that it was me who had helped catch the thief, and Paige was acting like I was the greatest hero of all time, smiling at me with her perfectly lip-glossed lips. She even let me wear that necklace during language arts— and I pretended that I hadn't ever touched it before.

I was like the new kid at school all over again, but this time I had a chance for a whole new set of friends.

"Where did you say you were from again?" Paige asked as I handed her back the necklace.

I looked at her coyly. "Oh, lots of places. But I really like it here."

Paige leaned onto my desk, put her chin in her hands, and smiled. "Why don't you wear your hair back, Ronnie? You have the greatest green eyes." She offered me a tie-back from her purse.

"Thanks."

"No problem. You saved my life today. My parents would have killed me if I'd lost that necklace. They told me not to wear it to school."

Pretty soon it was the end of the day and everyone was hurrying through the halls to catch their buses. It felt like everything was going to be okay, except when I passed the front office. I could see Cat through the glass window, sitting alone by the office-ladies. She was probably waiting for the vice principal to talk to her.

She must have sensed me standing there because suddenly she turned around and began staring at me with those sad eyes of hers, and I knew all at once that everything *wasn't* going to be okay.

A part of me wanted to go into the office, put my arms around her, and say, "Too bad you got in trouble," because, truly, I felt *terrible* inside, but I knew nothing I could say would make it right.

I started thinking about what a lowly sinner I had become.

A liar and a thief, I had betrayed my only friend.

But then, just as I was feeling my lowest, I spied Paige standing inside the front entrance to the school. It seemed like she was waiting for someone, which wasn't easy because all the kids were rushing by her, trying to get through the door.

Then I discovered that the person she was waiting for . . . was **me.**

As soon as she saw me, Paige called out in her perfectly warm and wonderful voice: "Hurry the hell up, Ronnie. Come sit with me on the bus."

October 25

Things have been great lately. I've been hanging out with Paige and her friends and learning what it's like to be popular. I still can't believe I'm popular because I've never fit in anywhere before. But this is exactly what I've become, thanks to Paige, ever since that thing happened with Cat stealing the necklace. That's how I like to think about it now, that *Cat* actually stole it, so I don't get mixed up in case anybody asks. But Cat is the only one who keeps asking.

"Who do you think put that necklace in my locker?" she asks at least once a week. She knows that I turned in the note to Miss Riley—and she says she doesn't blame me—but for some reason she hasn't connected that *I* was the one who *put* the necklace there. She also can't understand why I'm hanging around with someone like Paige. "I thought we both agreed we hated her," she'll say. Mostly, when she says that I try to change the subject or ignore her, but that makes me feel especially bad.

But not as bad as I felt when I got home from school today and overheard Alison talking on the phone in the kitchen.

"She's not ready," Alison said in a worried tone. "It's

much too soon. I can't see her being uprooted again so quickly. I mean, she's barely getting used to being *here*."

When she looked at me with this guilty expression on her face, I realized that she was talking about *me*, not one of her patients.

Grabbing a muffin out of the bowl on the table, I whispered, "Who's that?"

Alison covered the receiver with her hand. "It's Midge. She says she's found a permanent foster family who wants to . . . *meet* you."

I took a soda from the refrigerator and slammed the door so hard that it popped open again and Alison had to close it. Then I went into the other room to watch TV, turning it up overly loud on purpose. I was trying not to think about what she'd just told me. Was I getting dumped again? Just when I was finally fitting in?

That night as we ate dinner, Alison explained the reasons why this foster placement might be a wonderful opportunity. She stressed that I shouldn't interpret it as simply another rejection (by her) and that I must remember that this had been the plan all along—to get me ready for another, potentially permanent, family. She had taken me in as a favor to Midge because of all the referrals Alison got from their agency. Like she'd told me from the beginning, her house was only *temporary*.

"But I don't want to rush you out the door," she said. "Honestly, Midge thinks she knows you better than I do!"

Alison wasn't sure I'd made enough progress, but Midge didn't agree. This family, the Wagners, Midge said, was too perfect to pass up. "Tom's a surgeon! Laura's a dentist! And they love kids, especially teenagers. I can't believe her luck!" she had told Alison.

"They live nearby, so we could keep in touch if you'd like," Alison added as she poured me another glass of milk. "But if you think you're not ready," she repeated, "maybe I can convince Midge to let you stay."

What was I supposed to say? The Wagners could be *permanent*. I was tired of moving from place to place. Did I really have much of a choice?

"Do they have a dog?" I asked, spooning a pile of baked beans into my mouth.

My mother had promised that she would get me a dog someday. A dog would be someone I could talk to if things weren't working out. A dog would be awesome.

"Would it matter?" Alison asked.

"It might."

Alison looked puzzled. "I'm not sure. But they sound like the kind of family who'd get one for you, if they don't already have one." She got up from the table and brought her plate over to the sink. She turned on the small TV in the kitchen and put on the six o'clock news.

I sat there drinking my glass of milk. "Well, they live in the richest part of town, right?"

"I assume so," she replied, a bit exasperated. "They're both doctors."

I started thinking about how much closer I would be to Paige and the others with a new-and-improved address. Maybe the Wagners lived right on Penn Avenue!

"Okay," I said. "I'll go."

If she was going to dump me anyway, I might as well pretend I didn't care.

"Huh?" Alison seemed surprised. "You won't mind? It will be another big adjustment."

"No, it sounds like fun."

October 30

Alison and I had hardly any time together the rest of the week, between me hanging out with my new friends and Alison's appointments with her patients. What little time we did spend together felt forced somehow, like neither one of us could push out the words for what we were truly feeling. I gave up on doing my chores and began leaving dirty dishes around the house, but Alison didn't nag me. It was like we'd both stopped trying.

Midge arrived promptly at two thirty today, right after I got home from school.

"She's here!" Alison called up the stairs. I hurried to join them in the hall. I'd dressed in one of the newer outfits Alison had bought me at the Berkshire Mall, a short corduroy miniskirt (in taupe) with a matching sweater. My hair, shoulder-length now, was brushed back neatly behind a plaid headband. I wanted to make a good first impression.

I remember the day I met Alison. I'd been sitting on a splintery farmhouse porch, in shorts that were way too small, with my trusty black Hefty bag by my side. "Can't anyone afford to buy this poor girl a suitcase?" I'd heard Alison ask Midge as they walked toward me from the van.

"We have," Midge had answered. "She won't use them."

Midge was right. I won't. That's because people who use suitcases are coming back home. It would mean I had a place to come back *to*.

And I don't. Not yet. (I wonder if I ever will.)

Midge was waiting anxiously in Alison's hallway. She

twisted the big turquoise ring on her thumb, and ran her fingers through her thinning red hair. "I hope everything's in there," she said, nodding toward my bag on the rug by the front door.

Alison forced a smile. "If we've forgotten anything I can always bring it down to your office later."

"Wonderful," said Midge, a little too cheerily. "Then we're all set."

"I guess this is good-bye," said Alison sadly, putting out her soft arms to give me a hug. Her eyes looked moist.

Ever since my mother left me I've never been good at good-byes, and most of the time when I've had to leave a foster home it hasn't exactly been under the best of circumstances.

I felt shaky all of a sudden. Unsure.

I allowed Alison's hug for a brief second, then pulled away, not daring to look at her face. I was worried she might get emotional, like start crying or something, and that was the last thing I needed. Alison reached over to help with my bag, but I grabbed for it just as Midge opened the front door, and we quickly walked outside.

Out of the corner of my eye I watched poor Alison standing on her porch, dabbing at her nose with a tissue, hoping, I guess, that I would at least turn around and wave.

But I just couldn't. After all, she was the one who was dumping me.

I didn't tell anyone at school that I was moving, but I made up a story just in case about this new family (the Wagners) being my true, biological relatives, and how they had just come back from France. This would become the real reason why I had to move into that big, beautiful house on Penn Avenue. Now I would fit in with them even better. I couldn't wait!

After we left Alison's, Midge was all chatty like we were going to the mall to buy me a new outfit—not driving to meet my new future family!

"I just know you're going to *love* them," Midge said as we went up and down those hilly side streets in town.

Unexpectedly, I got kind of sad. I wondered if Alison would miss me. I pictured her gray-brown eyes with their soft wrinkles on either side. Alison's eyes always seemed accepting and wise—probably because she's helped so many people. I've never known anyone with a kinder face.

I guess I'd gotten distracted thinking about Alison and was only half listening to all of Midge's blah-blah talking because suddenly I noticed we weren't in Liberty anymore. Midge was pulling out onto the highway and passing right by the mall—heading clear out of town!

As we slowed down in traffic, we passed one of those black Amish buggies—a horse-drawn carriage with blinking, modern taillights on the back. It was such a contrast to the passing traffic, I thought: a clashing of old worlds with new.

I figured maybe we had to stop by Midge's house as we sometimes did to let out her dog or to pick up my files, so I checked, just to make sure. "Hey, Midge?" I asked. "Why are we going this way?"

She looked surprised. "Hon, you know this is the way to Lancaster, don't you?"

"Why are we going to *Lancaster*?" I asked with a tone. Lancaster was just about the *last* place I wanted to go.

Midge seemed confused. "Didn't Alison tell you? The Wagners *live* in Lancaster."

"No!"

Of course Alison didn't tell me the Wagners lived in Lancaster.

And neither did Midge!

I started to panic. I swear I was going to have my very first panic attack right there in the car. My heart felt like it was beating out of my chest! Talk about not having any control over your destiny! I couldn't believe this was happening. After I'd *finally* found a place where people liked me for once in my life, she was telling me I had to give it all up! To go back to the very town where all those horrible things had happened to me.

I was finding it very hard to breathe.

Suddenly I went back to the time right after I got put into foster care. It was the middle of sixth grade. I was being jerked around to all of these different foster homes. I was miserable. Angry. If anyone teased me about the littlest thing, I would completely flip out, throwing things, cursing.

One of the kids at school used to call me Foster Freak. He thought that was funny until I threw a chunk of snow at him (with a rock inside it) and he had to wear a patch over his eye for a month.

(That's why I don't tell many people about my past.)

At one of my worst homes, they took in six of us kids, plus they had three of their own. And seventeen cats. They kept the heat so low in February (like about fifty degrees) that we had to sleep three to a bed to stay warm. I slept with a handicapped girl named Carly, and her sister Crystal (whose real mom had once locked them in a cage). Flea-infested cats would jump on us in the middle of the night and wrap themselves around our feet. Flea bites itch like crazy; I scratched my ankles till they bled.

Thinking about it (even now in the car), made my ankle start to itch.

I looked over at Midge.

Didn't she realize that all of those memories were stuck back in Lancaster, waiting to suffocate me? And that's not even counting my mom leaving me, my uncle and Raylene kicking me out, and, of course, what Kenny did to our family.

Oh. My. God.

Midge exited the highway.

I opened the window to get some air. "You don't seriously expect me to live in Lancaster, do you? Are you forgetting all that's happened there?"

Midge looked annoyed, but she kept driving anyway, trying to convince me how happy I could be with this new family. I hated her right then, so I slumped in the seat, put on my headphones, and turned up the volume extra loud.

When we got to the Wagners, I refused to get out of the van, but Midge forced me by threatening to dump my bag all over the street (she knew that would get me). She tried to guide me up the sidewalk to their house— which wasn't nearly as big or glamorous as I'd expected. It was a regular-sized white Colonial with a wraparound front porch.

"You're being ridiculous," Midge said, with a nervous smile stretched across her face. "Teenagers are almost impossible to place. Don't you realize how *lucky* you are?"

Lucky? I didn't feel lucky at all.

I felt trapped!

I had to do something.

So I sat down on the sidewalk and refused to go another step. Then I began to scream and bite myself and pull out my hair (just a few strands) while Midge searched her purse for a cigarette. She ignored me so I began to roll on the ground. Thrashing back and forth— and moaning.

While I was thrashing around, I noticed that the door to the house had opened and the Wagners (a man in a suit and a woman with a blue dress) were watching me like I was having some kind of nervous break- down—which, come to think of it, maybe I was. They stood there silently on their front porch, shading their eyes from the afternoon sun.

"Get up!" Midge yelled.

"No!"

"Fine," Midge sputtered, "then don't meet them! I don't care. Go wait in the van while I try to explain." I picked myself up, pulled down my skirt, and hopped quickly back into the van.

She spent about half an hour talking to the Wagners on their porch, which was decorated with piles of different-sized pumpkins. And she kept checking on me (like every ten minutes) to make sure I didn't want to change my mind. "Do you understand the implica- tions?" she asked. "This might be your very last chance."

"I just can't," I said, determined not to stay. "Too many bad things have happened to me here."

So finally, in the end, we left.

"They were very disappointed," Midge told me as she got into the van. "But they certainly didn't want to cause any *more* trauma in your life." She related this to me with a real attitude, like implying that I was being so ungrateful.

I didn't say another word to her the whole time she was driving us back to Liberty, but as we crossed over the small bridge into town, I got sort of carsick wondering what would happen next.

When we drove past Cat's house, two blocks over from Alison's, I could see the TV flickering through her bedroom window upstairs. During the summer we had sat in her room almost every day, watching soap operas and MTV together. But ever since the necklace incident I hadn't been over there at all—not even once. That suddenly made me feel guilty and awful—like the worst friend *ever*. I guessed I deserved whatever bad things were about to happen to me.

When we got to Alison's house, it was dark. Midge knocked on the door, but she wasn't home. Where the heck could Alison be on a Friday night? She never seemed to do anything fun when I was around.

As we waited in Midge's van in front of the house, Midge kept getting out to make private calls on her cell phone. "I just reached Alison," she finally said, shutting the door. "She'll be here soon. You realize that she might not want you back?"

"Yeah, right," I said. What did she expect me to say? It was getting long past dark and my stomach was making these gurgling noises because I was starving, but I think I was worried, too. What *would* happen if Alison said no?

We had to wait like *forever* for the headlights of Alison's car to finally pull behind us on the street— but before that happened, I spent some serious time thinking in the backseat of Midge's van.

Here I was, once again, on the edge of having no place to go. I had strayed off the path; that was crystal clear. I figured God was punishing me and trying to give me a message at the same time. When Alison had asked if I minded going to the Wagners, I could have said, "Yes, I do mind. I like it here; *I want to stay.*"

But I didn't say that. Instead, I acted like it didn't bother me in the least. Maybe it had kind of pissed me off that she would give me up so easily, but mostly all I had thought about was the chance to be rich like Paige.

So, obviously none of this would've happened if I hadn't been so greedy. Like wanting to be popular *and* rich. Why couldn't just being popular be good enough?

That's when I made a deal. If Alison would let me stay, then I promised God I would try to be a better person. I would try to be good again, just like I used to be. (It might be a good idea to make it up to Cat somehow too.)

I would figure out a way to be so good that all that goodness would make its way all the way up to Alaska, and my mother would feel it and know it deep in her heart, and then she would come get me and take me there to live with her forever (or at least until I was eighteen). So I prayed and prayed really hard for about ten minutes while Alison and Midge decided what to do.

When they finally told me I could get out of the van, I said to Alison, "Do you know when you get lost in the woods or something? They tell you how important it is to stay in one place? To not move around a lot, so they can find you?"

I don't know why I said that except I felt like I was lost most of the time, and I guess a part of me wanted to be found. I was sort of crying too, I mean, what if she *didn't* want me? I had hardly said good-bye, and had treated her pretty badly when I was there, throwing cans at her and stealing.

But then Alison looked at me with those beautiful gray-brown eyes and nodded, like she **completely** understood.

"You want to stay here with me."

Like it wasn't even a question.

Midge told us that they were suspending all future foster home placements until Alison determined that I was completely ready. I glanced at Alison and she was smiling like, sure, that's what she'd wanted in the first place.

Alison's house looked so welcoming. The outside light was on and it made a quiet glow on the stoop. She had a gigantic jack-o'-lantern sitting there on the steps that we had carved together last weekend, and I thought to myself, gee, I guess I'll be here for Halloween after all.

Alison grinned as she picked up my bag. "Let's get you settled," she said. Then she put her arm around me and we walked together toward the house. Before we got to the door, I glanced up. The curve of the moon hung all golden in the sky—sort of like a hammock for the stars.

November 4

Here are Paige's screen names: **sexygurl**, **pageme**
Britnee's: **bedroomeyes**
Sarika's: **desertflower**

Cat's: **purrfect**
Mine: **heartrampled** (maybe I should change it?)

I have to call or IM Paige every night to find out who we are going to talk to the next day—or rather who we *aren't*; meaning, who Paige is pissed at now.

Paige doesn't come right out and say it, but she definitely expects me to check with her about certain things. And if I don't, or if I dress the wrong way or talk to the wrong person, she will make some sort of comment or give me a mean look.

I guess it's when she stops saying things that you're in trouble.

Like yesterday, in between first and second period, when we passed Cat in the hallway. I waved to Cat and said, "Hey," which I've started doing again to try to make it up to her, when Paige immediately stopped walking and grabbed my arm really tight.

"Ronnie, please don't make me say this again."

"Huh?"

"Cat's a weirdo. A loser. Pick a side and stay there."

Later, when I told Cat I couldn't say hello to her anymore, at least not in school, she shrugged. "Do what you have to," she said, but her needy eyes were peeking out from behind her black bangs, so I promised we could still hang out together at home, at least once in a while . . . *maybe* . . . as long as nobody found out.

I asked Alison first thing the morning after I got back from the Wagners if we could get a dog. What I really said was, "Alison, I think you should get a dog."

She replied, "Why on earth would I want to do something crazy like that?"

I told her so that when I left again she would have somebody to keep her company. She hugged me and said, "But, dear, I don't like dogs. And you're not going anywhere for a long, long time."

That made me feel good, but sort of nervous, too, so I wanted to make sure we were on the same page. "Not until my mother comes for me, right?"

She looked at me kind of sad. "Right. Of course not. Not until then."

I guess Alison changed her mind because we went to the animal shelter that very afternoon and got Lucky. He is the best dog ever! He's a border collie mix. We're not sure what else he's mixed with. I love him *soooo* much!

He's black and white with a black mark above his right eye that looks kind of like a comma—and he's always smiling. He makes the funniest expressions and he even sneezes and gets the hiccups—just like a real person.

We have to get him trained, though, 'cause he keeps chewing stuff and jumping up on things and "shitting in the house." (Alison's words, not mine.)

"Did you take him out?" Alison will ask, and I will tell her, "Of course," even though I do forget occasionally.

Then Alison will look all confused. "The lady said he was house-trained. Why does he keep *shitting in the house*?"

"Maybe he's nervous about being in a new environment."

(I know about that sort of thing.)

Alison's signed us up for obedience lessons. Puppy Kindergarten is what they call it, starting next Saturday.

It's in the morning, which is a good thing because all the girls are going to the mall in the afternoon—all the popular girls, that is.

Not Cat, because she's not invited, because she's not popular, because all of us have to ignore her, because of Paige.

But it's really hard to ignore Cat at the bus stop in the morning when she's standing there looking all alone and chubby in her too-tight pants. And it's hard to ignore her when she's sitting all by herself in the cafeteria or getting a drink of water at the water fountain in the hall—but now I'm part of that circle that needs to shut out kids like her.

I have to laugh extra loud when they make fun of her; it's expected.

The truth is that a part of me actually misses hanging out with Cat 'cause she's the only one here who I've told about my past. Her family is pretty messed up, even though it looks almost normal from the outside. Her mom's been in rehab (like my mom), and I think her mom's boyfriend has been in jail.

When Cat looks at me with her hurt, dark eyes—as if she wishes things could go back to the way they were before—I feel awful.

But honestly, what can I do?

November 14

As we drove up the winding road on Saturday morning, the hills around Dog-Ear Farm were lit up with the last colors of fall. The sky was a sort of true blue, with high puffy clouds that were reflected in the dark water of the pond. The parking lot was behind the pond, and behind that was a tall, barnlike building where we would have our first obedience training lesson for Lucky. Alison said it was a beautiful spot with a priceless view, which, in her opinion, was utterly wasted on dogs.

"Dogs deserve nice surroundings too," I replied. Even after almost two weeks with Lucky, Alison still is not crazy about dogs. I'm hoping he'll grow on her.

After we'd only been inside for a few minutes, Lucky had already piddled on the floor and was scratching his way toward the door. He was terrified of the other dogs—and of most of the people, too.

Our dog training instructor, a lady with dyed-blond hair and an eyebrow piercing, sized him up right away. "Hi. I'm *Star*," she said, introducing herself. "You got your dog at the shelter, right?"

Alison and I looked at each other.

How did she know?

"He's undersocialized. I can always tell. Did they tell you he'd been abused? He's going to need tons of work."

Alison blinked three times, like maybe getting Lucky had been a big mistake. (Like maybe he was untrainable.) I knew what happened to those kinds of dogs; I decided to pay close attention in class.

For our first exercise, we had to put our dogs on the leash and walk them in a circle around the room. We were supposed to say, "Heel! Heel!"

As I pulled and tugged and dragged on Lucky's leash so we could keep up with the others, the door to the training room suddenly opened and something incredible happened. Standing there, like he had dropped down from the sky, was Francis, the youth director from my old church!

He looked almost the same to me, maybe just a little older. I'd moved to another foster home right before his fiftieth birthday party last year. He was wearing a pink tie-dyed T-shirt and a pair of khaki pants with sandals. I couldn't have been more surprised—or happy!

"Sorry we're late," he said as his dog, a golden retriever puppy, bounded into the room. Francis glanced around the room politely, but when he saw me he got the biggest smile on his face—and then he waved!

I quickly handed the leash to Alison and ran over, hugging him tight. He smelled like that spicy aftershave he always wears. I was so happy to see him I got tears in my eyes. "What are *you* doing here?" he asked, grinning.

"I'm with my new foster mom," I said, pointing across the room. "Alison just got me a dog!"

Francis must have noticed the nervous look on Alison's face; he said that I should go back to her and Lucky—and that we could talk more at break time.

"Who is that guy? Do you know him?" Alison asked anxiously when I returned.

Did she think I was in the habit of hugging strange men?

"Excuse me?" I said sarcastically.

"I meant, *how* do you know him, dear?"

I told her how I had first met Francis when I was with another foster family at church last year, and how he was the nicest youth minister—*ever*. "So I'd appreciate it if you'd chill, okay?"

Then we moved on to the next activity, which was teaching Lucky to lie down. While we were practicing, Francis came over to join us. His puppy immediately jumped up on Alison, startling her. "Oh,

I'm so sorry. Get down, Checkers! What's your dog's name, Ronnie? He's shy, right? But awfully sweet."

"We call him Lucky. It was on his tag when they found him."

"Well, he sure is *lucky* to have you in his life," Francis said to me, but his eyes lit up when he glanced at Alison. He stuck out his hand, giving her his warmest smile.

"Alison, right?"

"Is it *Father* Francis?" She smoothed down her long denim skirt, and adjusted the charm bracelet on her wrist.

"Oh, no," he told her. "I'm only the youth minister. Just Francis."

Francis was Alison's exact height, but much wider, with what you might call a barrel chest. The top of his head was bald, but he had a circular patch of dark curly hair that always reminded me of the ceramic bank my uncle kept in my mother's old bedroom. The bank was the figure of a monk in a brown robe, with a white rope-tie around his waist. On the front of the robe were the words, "Thou shalt not steal."

(That was one commandment I always seemed to have trouble with.)

Just as we were getting reacquainted, Star said it was time for the dogs' bathroom break, so we went outside and stood together near a tall pine tree. I remembered all the great youth group trips I'd taken with Francis, and how he was always there to listen if I had a problem.

"What's happening with Ronnie's mother?" he asked, directing his question to Alison. "Is she still in the picture?"

I closed my eyes as I remembered our last phone call.

"So how are you doing at saving money, Mom?"

"You can't keep pressuring me to bring you up here, Ronnie. It's not good for my nerves. Shit. I'm doing the best I can!"

"Midge monitors their contact," Alison replied, shrugging. "She's making sporadic progress, I guess."

"Ah, yes," he said knowingly. "Sporadic was always the case."

Alison seemed to frown when he said that. I could almost hear her thinking, is he another person who thinks he knows more about you than I do?

After a few minutes, Alison's cell phone started ringing and she went to her car to take the call. I stayed behind and tried to describe to Francis what I'd been doing since we'd last seen each other. It seemed like forever ago. I left out any of the bad things I'd done, because it mattered, I guess, what he thought of me. He asked me about going to church again. Now that I might be in one place for a while, I told him that sounded like a great idea.

It couldn't have been more than ten minutes when Star clapped her hands. "We're out of time! See you all next week!"

Alison began walking toward us from the car. "Is it over already?" she asked, pulling her purse over her shoulder. "I guess we should get going."

I couldn't help feeling disappointed. It had been so nice being with Francis again; I didn't want it to end. Before we got to our car, Francis reached into his back pocket and handed Alison a business card from his wallet.

"Don't hesitate to call me," he said. "Anytime. Night or day."

She looked puzzled by his offer.

He smiled and winked at me. "You seem like a nice person, Alison. I don't want our Ronnie to wear you out."

"Hey," I said, punching him playfully on the arm. "Thanks a lot."

Francis laughed his great chuckling laugh while Alison studied the card for a second before she dropped it into her purse.

"I'll see *you* next week," he said, tousling my hair. He whistled and Checkers jumped into the front seat of his car.

On the way home, I was talking rapid-fire about how awesome it had been seeing Francis and how it was God working one of his many miracles again, I was sure of it. "And he's going to get someone to bring me to church! I can go to youth group again on Wednesday nights!"

"What? A stranger? I would have taken you! Why didn't you ask me?"

"I don't know. It's no big deal."

"I just signed you up for tennis lessons on Wednesday nights," she said, sounding annoyed. "You also have homework, meetings with Midge, orthodontist appointments, and now this dog training. How are we supposed to fit all that in?"

What was her problem?

"I thought you'd be happy for me!"

"I am. But he should have checked with me first," she said. "Who does he think has to coordinate your busy schedule?"

We crossed the two-lane bridge into Liberty, about

a mile from the house. "Oh, probably he thought he'd tell you about it next week."

"Sure. Probably," she said.

Alison was quiet. I wrapped my arms around Lucky, giving him another hug. "It was so good to see Francis. Lucky liked him, didn't you, boy?"

I snuck a sideways glance at her. "You know he's single, Alison, just like you. Maybe you should hook up with him."

"Ronnie! Don't talk like that. He's like a *minister!*"

"Please. He curses just like you. Besides he's a *youth* minister. It's not the same thing. He was married once, you know, but his wife died a couple of years ago."

She glanced at me again.

"I think he likes you," I added. "He definitely was . . . you know . . . *interested.*"

Alison made a face, like, *please.*

She pulled into the driveway and popped open the trunk to get out the heavy bag of dog food we had bought at the supermarket earlier. I opened the car door for Lucky, and he trotted through the garage.

Alison followed, lugging the heavy bag. "Wait a minute," she said.

"What?"

"Before you start any matchmaking schemes, Ronnie, I want to tell you something. Even if your friend Francis *was* interested," she explained, "I happen to be involved at the moment. With somebody else."

"Really?"

I didn't know she had a boyfriend.

"With who?"

"With *you*, silly. And that's all the relationship I want—or have time for."

I rolled my eyes and let Lucky inside.

Later today

About ten minutes after we got home from Puppy Kindergarten, Cat was at our front doorstep, ringing the bell. She'd seen me yesterday afternoon running around with Lucky in our yard, and said she was just dying to meet our new puppy.

I told her to "Come on in," like I had invited her over, like things were back to normal—even though we hadn't actually hung out together in weeks.

Lucky was tuckered out from our busy morning. He took a nap in his favorite sunny spot on the Oriental rug near the bay window. Cat sat her butt down on the floor—I could see her belly rolls when she sat like that—and she petted him very gently behind the ears like I showed her, so he wouldn't get scared.

"He's *awesome*," she said. "I wish I could get another dog."

"Why don't you? King's getting old, right?" King was her bulgy-eyed pug.

"Right, but Bud would probably say, 'Are you crazy, girl? You don't take care of the goddamn dog we have.'" She said it in a low, southern drawl because Bud was from somewhere like West Virginia or Tennessee.

Cat made me laugh. I realized that I'd missed spending time with her. I felt bad that she couldn't stay any longer because I'd already made plans.

"You have to leave soon," I told her. "I said I'd go shopping with Paige."

"Okay. See you around," she said morosely. "I guess."

Why did she have to make me feel so guilty?

"Cat? What if I call you as soon as I get home?"

She perked right back up after I said that and asked if maybe I could sleep over tonight. When I asked Alison, she raised her eyebrows like, *maybe not*. Alison always worries that they have "supervision issues" at that house, but I told Cat I would call her anyway.

I met up with Paige and Britnee at the mall near the entrance to the Bon-Ton. After we each got an iced coffee at Starbucks, we walked over to Victoria's Secret because Paige wanted to get a new bra or a thong.

While Paige searched through the Wonderbras on the mini plastic hangers, Britnee and I laughed at the sexy underwear, which had strategically placed decorative features. We were having a good time until we got into the dressing room. Then it started to be *not* such a good time, as Paige shut the dressing room door behind us.

Paige tried on a black bra that made her look perfect, but she was complaining about how if she got this bra she wouldn't have any money left for a thong.

"Why don't we just do what we always do?" suggested Britnee.

I wondered what that could be.

Paige said, "Exactly." Pulling her long brown hair around her neck, she bent over and took out a pair of tiny scissors from the manicure kit in her purse. Kneeling, she expertly clipped the price tags from a black lacey thong that she had obviously sneaked into the dressing room. She stood up and handed the thong to me.

"Ronnie? I believe it's your turn."

I looked at her like, *are you crazy*?

"You actually expect me to *steal* this for you?" I asked. "From a *store*?"

This was serious, way different from when I would occasionally "borrow" minor things at Alison's house—or even when I put that necklace in Cat's locker. This was *shoplifting*!

Didn't she understand what she was asking me to do? What would happen if I got caught?

"Come on," Paige replied. "Don't be such a baby. We do it all the time. This is what we *do* when we go shopping."

Britnee nodded. "It's easy once you get used to it. We get all sorts of neat stuff—for free."

Wow. I looked at both of their faces and realized that I didn't have a choice.

I *had* to do this if I wanted to stay friends with them.

Then it was almost like some other girl, not me, slipped the thong into the front pocket of her jeans, pulled her shirt down over the top of it, and tried to make it look casual as she walked out of the store.

It took some convincing, but Alison agreed to let me sleep over at Cat's that night, even though I hadn't ever slept there before. I told her to relax, that Cat's mom would be home by nine thirty, and I would only be one tiny little block away. Alison's eyebrows still had that worried look. "I trust you to call me, Ronnie. If there's *any* problem. Any problem *at all*."

I'd forgotten how much I liked being over at Cat's. It is Alison's exact house inside—except her living room is where our kitchen is and vice versa. But you don't have to worry as much about where you leave your stuff at Cat's house. We don't have to throw out our soda cans right away since there are always half-empty cans sitting on countertops and tables. And there are piles of magazines and stacks of catalogs all over the place. Obviously, Cat's mom is not a neat freak like Alison, and she leaves Cat alone a lot, for instance, when she works or when she goes out to listen to Bud's band, so we pretty much have the whole place to ourselves.

The first thing we did was go up to her bedroom. Cat has a daybed, so it feels like you're sitting on a couch, and her comforter is black (actually most of her room is black, but it's cozy in there—sort of like a cave). She brought up a Mike's Hard Lemonade (which is lemonade with a kick) from the refrigerator downstairs and offered me a sip.

I felt kind of guilty about drinking, since Alison had trusted me, but Cat said, "Just take a few sips. You're sleeping over. Alison will never know." She pulled a magazine from under her bed and then we did a sex survey from *Hot Teens*.

These were Cat's answers:

Favorite drink to get you in the mood: "Mike's Hard Lemonade."

Hottest Guy you *haven't* kissed: "That's easy. Tyler Miller."

"But Paige likes him," I said.

"Okay, then Jon."

I didn't have the heart to tell her—Jon makes fun of her all the time.

Sexiest color: "Black."

Hottest TV show: "*The Real World* on MTV."

"Doing the nasty" position you'd like to try soon: (We laughed at that one.)

Sexiest piece of underwear in your drawer:

Underwear? This got me thinking about thongs, and all of a sudden I threw the magazine onto the floor. We'd both been laughing, but my laughing stopped as I remembered what had happened this afternoon. I began telling Cat about stealing the thong and how bad I felt, especially since I was planning to ask Alison to take me to church tomorrow, and how my whole body was shaking when I had to walk past the can-I-help-you-please? saleslady without getting caught, and how if I had gotten caught I would probably be at juvenile detention this very moment instead of chilling in Cat's bedroom with a Mike's.

Then, I guess because I was feeling extra emotional from drinking, I leaned back on her pillow and told her about everything else, too. It all came spilling out: how Paige and Britnee always make fun of her behind her back and how badly I feel when I have to laugh right along with them, and even—this part was the scariest!—the part about taking Paige's necklace and putting it into Cat's locker!

I didn't want her to think I was an awful person, but I also knew that if I ever hoped to be forgiven, she needed to know the total, absolute truth.

"It was a terrible thing to do. I don't know why I did it. At first I wanted you to have the necklace, 'cause I knew you liked it. But then Miss Riley was forcing me to tell her, like she'd already figured it out . . . and I didn't want to get in trouble! They would have sent me away! And afterward, I guess, Paige wanted to be friends with me. Please, please, don't hate me."

Cat didn't say anything. She just looked at me quietly with those dark, sad eyes of hers until I was ready to scream. "Say something!" I said. "Call me a bitch. *Anything!*"

But Cat didn't call me a bitch. She didn't even seem mad. After a few seconds, all she said was, "You must really want to be friends with them—to do all those things. Especially if it makes you feel so bad inside."

I let out a deep sigh. "Dude, you have no idea."

We went back to watching TV, until later, when she came up with this totally crazy idea. "Do you want to go down to the basement and look at Bud's gun collection?"

Gun collection?

"Are you serious? I don't *think* so," I replied. Because even the idea of just *one* gun being in her house totally freaked me out.

"Gee, Ronnie. What's the big deal?" She looked at me kind of weird. "Don't you think you kind of *owe* me?"

So that's why I stood in the kitchen at the top of her creepy basement stairs, waiting for her to flick on the light.

"Be careful; don't lock it behind you," she warned, pausing on the top stair. "Or we can't get out."

I nodded, checked the handle twice, and followed her down the stairs.

Cat's basement had a low ceiling like Alison's, but it felt smaller on account of Bud's band equipment being down there, drums and amps and old dusty crates, and also because it was only lit by one dim lightbulb hanging on a string.

Cat knew the exact place where he kept them, above the red cabinet behind the furnace. She stood on a box, reached over her head, and took a gun out of the case. "This is the one he used to shoot that guy."

Oh my God! "Bud *shot* somebody?"

"A *long* time ago. Self-defense," she explained, like it was nothing. "Here. Hold it." She practically forced the gun into my hand. "Isn't it cool?"

It had a wooden handle with dull, silver metal everywhere else. The gun was heavier than I thought it would be and felt strangely powerful, almost like it had a life of its own. "It feels like it could start shooting without me even pulling the trigger."

Cat laughed. "It's not loaded," she said, "but I know where he hides the bullets."

I quickly gave it back to her, making sure to point it down at the floor.

She couldn't take her eyes off it . . . and neither could I.

Suddenly we heard a noise that sounded like it was coming from the kitchen. She said it was probably her older brother getting home from work and looking for something to eat. She put the gun back in its hiding place and we hurried back upstairs.

After that we watched some TV and she gulped down another bottle of Mike's, but I said I didn't want any more. Her mother came home, peeked into the room, and said good night. When we got tired, we lined up our sleeping bags real close to each other on the floor. Cat gave me one of her favorite stuffed teddy bears to sleep with and turned out the light.

I couldn't fall asleep at first—there were too many strange noises in her house. I heard a pitter-patter like a mouse in the attic, and a motorcycle drive by, and voices sounding like Bud and Cat's mom arguing downstairs. When I finally fell asleep, I had a dream that someone was chasing me. They had a knife or a gun or some kind of weapon. It was pretty scary. But the scariest thing was that I couldn't tell if I had done something wrong and deserved to be chased—or whether I was innocent and just trying to get away.

November 15

It was so nice to sit next to Francis and some kids from the youth group at church this morning. We had snacks in the meeting room after the service. When Alison picked me up she asked how church went, and I told her okay, and she said she'd been thinking that I needed to start sharing with her the bad things I remember happening before my mother left me—and after my mother left me, like at my uncle's house, in foster care, *everything*!

"The past has a way of catching up with us," Alison said. "And I only know what I've read in your file. It's Sunday. We have nothing planned. Let's go out to lunch and talk."

"Some things are hard to talk about," I said nervously.

"But wouldn't it feel good to let some of that go?"

I told her "I guess," but the words wouldn't come. So after lunch she said that I could show her what I've written on my computer instead. "You only need to show me a page or two," she suggested, "when you feel comfortable."

She was stressing the word *when*.

"Okay," I answered. "Maybe." But I was thinking probably not.

I am stressing the words *probably not*.

I suppose she wants me to tell her how I haven't seen my "father" since right after my mother left me near the end of fifth grade. It was at the custody hearing that he made his appearance. My caseworker (another one, not Midge) and I had waited outside on those sunny marble steps at the courthouse in Lancaster. My "father" approached us before the hearing, wearing a Harley-Davidson T-shirt and dirty cutoff jeans.

You'd think I would be trying to memorize his face, since I'd only seen him once when I was three, but I couldn't tear my eyes away from his fingernails, which were bitten to the quick and stained with ink and oil. The only thing he said was, "Sorry. There's no way I can take care of you."

(He had just gotten out of jail.)

"I can barely support my own sorry-ass self," he added. "Never mind a half-*growed*, eleven-year-old kid."

He actually said *growed*.

What a loser!

I never want to see him again.

So I remained in the custody of my mother's only brother (who was fifty-two) and his girlfriend, Raylene, which is what my mother had arranged—right before she left.

At the apartment where I'd lived with my mother there was always lots of activity. The phone was constantly ringing. Strange people came in and out, even in the middle of the night, knocking on the door three times, *rap, rap, rap*, which meant they were there to buy drugs from Kenny. I was afraid sometimes, and busy picking up after all their friends (throwing away beer bottles or old pizza boxes) or doing chores. There were my brothers to play with and Kenny to stay away from.

It was quiet at my uncle's house in the country and things happened at a slower pace. Nobody seemed to knock on my uncle's door, especially not at night. I hate to sound ungrateful, but it was kind of . . . *dull*. They lived in the middle of nowhere and there was no one to play with and Raylene expected me to know how to entertain myself and it annoyed her when I didn't.

I can remember exactly what my room looked like back then, which was my mother's room when she was a little girl (my uncle moved in after Grandpa died). It had a pink chenille bedspread, the bank shaped like a monk on the shelf, and a window that looked out over five or six junk cars and a pile of tires in the neighbor's backyard.

Nighttime, especially, I missed my mom the most—even more than I miss her now, if that's possible. I missed my little brothers, too. I would lie under my pink bedspread every night before falling asleep, wondering what awful thing I had done to make them leave me behind.

You have to give my mother credit, though—she tried to keep in touch. She would call me at my uncle's house from wherever she was—Saturday nights were her routine. Around seven.

But if she didn't call, I'd get really upset. Those nights were the hardest. Was she still alive? Were my brothers okay? Would I ever hear from her again?

Even if she *did* remember to call, I'd get upset. It was so hard to listen to her trying-to-be-happy-sounding voice on the phone. She would ask me, "How's things?" and what was I supposed to tell her?

That Raylene was nasty? And Uncle Melvin was old and sick? That they had doctors' appointments practically every day, so I could never invite any of my friends over to play? That I hated every single minute in that stupid, boring house?

Then Mom would put Derek or Dan on the phone, and all I could think about was how unfair it was that she'd picked my brothers to go with her instead of me. After our calls I would get so mad sometimes that I'd throw things around my room or bang my head against the wall. Or the next morning I'd hide in the bathroom—right before we were set to leave for church.

Raylene, with her silky church dresses and wide-brimmed church hats, didn't like that one bit; she stomped and yelled and fussed, but I didn't care. Maybe they'd get tired of me and send me to Alaska—that's what I was hoping for. So I'd lock myself in the bathroom for hours. I'd refuse to take a bath or wash my hair.

I didn't like upsetting Uncle Melvin, but it was kind of fun getting to Raylene, watching her heavy cross pendant swing angrily below her fleshy neck. It gave me a powerful feeling, like making something happen—instead of waiting for bad things to happen to me.

Eventually, though, Raylene got fed up. "That is enough of that. We have to pray on this. This needs a praying solution."

She talked to her minister at church, and they decided that it was too upsetting for me (and them) to go through the calls from my mother week after week—it must be what was making me act "inappropriately." So we had to stop talking on the phone. Just like that. Postcards or letters only, from then on. No more calls. Period. End of story.

"It's God's will," was the way Raylene put it, and she made my uncle agree. Raylene also made me start praying in my room, morning and night, figuring the good Lord would help keep me from missing my mother so much. "But don't be praying for that good-for-nothing Kenny," she said. "Thank sweet Jesus that you're here with us. As I've told you before, that man deserves to go straight to hell."

Then one night, about a month later, in mid-December when I was in sixth grade, I remember saying I was going upstairs to do my praying before I went to sleep (at exactly nine o'clock, lights out!), but I'd actually decided to lie on my bed and look through the *Dog Fancy* magazine that Uncle Melvin had gotten me from the CVS. I was hoping for a dog for Christmas even though Raylene had said, "Over my dead body"—but I thought I had my uncle almost convinced.

I thought it would relax me, but looking at that magazine reminded me of how my brother Derek had always loved dogs, just like me. I wondered if Mom had gotten him one yet and when I would see them again. I felt so sad.

She and my brothers couldn't afford to come back for Christmas that year (that's what Uncle Melvin told me), and I hadn't seen them since they'd left last spring. And now I wasn't even allowed to hear Mom's lonely-sounding voice on the phone anymore. These things were too depressing to think about for very long. It made me feel hopeless and desperate.

In order to survive I knew I *had* to come up with a plan. Since my mother couldn't afford to come get me and Raylene would never agree to let me go, at least not while Kenny was living there, I decided that I would have to get the money myself—and run away.

All the way up to Alaska.

Luckily, I happened to know where my uncle kept most of his life savings. It was stashed in one of Raylene's oval hatboxes on the top shelf of their bedroom closet. (I'd found it one day when I was hiding there.) If I acted before I lost my nerve, I figured maybe I could make it to my mom's place by Christmas.

Uncle Melvin and Raylene were still downstairs watching TV—the ten o'clock news, like they always did before they went to bed. I tiptoed out of my bedroom on the creaky wooden floor of the hallway.

It was now or never!

With my socks sliding on the slippery floor, I dashed across to their bedroom, holding my breath.

The room was dark, but I didn't dare turn on the light. As soon as I opened the closet door, I knew the automatic light would pop on. I reached for the hatbox and set it down next to me. I lifted the lid and peeked inside. The money was still there, just as I'd remembered it. There were stacks of twenty-dollar bills bound together with pink rubber bands.

How much would it take to buy a plane ticket? Should I take a whole stack? Or just slip a bill out of every pile?

Unfortunately, just at that exact minute, Raylene must have decided to come upstairs early. I guess I was so busy counting the money that I didn't even hear her. She opened the bedroom door, flicked on the light, and caught me with the box wide open—and a fistful of bills in my hand.

Raylene screamed. "Oh my Lord, now this child's *stealing* from us too!"

Uncle Melvin hurried up the stairs, as fast as I'd ever seen him. He was angry and breathing hard. It scared me when he put his hand to his chest and almost stumbled. Raylene went over to the nightstand and handed him a pill, which he put under his tongue. He sat down on their bed and tried to catch his breath. Raylene was glaring at me like I better not move an inch.

In between crying, I tried to explain. "Mom can't turn me away if I show up on her doorstep, right? I'll pay you back, I promise. You've *got* to let me go."

After he was feeling better, my uncle pulled me onto his skinny lap. "The real reason you can't visit your mama, Veronica, is because she's been sent away. She got caught with drugs again. She's up there in jail. Six months' worth, I think."

"Don't think Kenny wants you up there, either," added Raylene. "He's having trouble with those boys all by himself."

I remembered how Kenny had practically kicked my mother across the kitchen one time because she'd forgotten to clean up the dirty dishes; I certainly didn't want to be taken care of by *him*.

Uncle Melvin rocked me on the bed as I sobbed into his arms. Raylene made me sleep on a pile of quilts on the floor of their room that night to make sure I didn't steal anything else. She called Children and Youth the very next day.

After the social worker got there, Raylene told him all about the fits I would throw, how I was always hiding in closets, and, of course, the stealing. She said their minister had warned that I might need more help than they could give me.

The social worker seemed worried. "That might be true."

He suggested that my uncle and Raylene attend parenting classes to help them learn how to deal with my issues, but Raylene said, "We don't need any parenting classes. We've been nothing but wonderful parents to this girl!"

Then something really terrible happened. Uncle Melvin told the social worker he was sorry, but he didn't think he could take care of me anymore. "I love my niece, but Raylene seems to think I'm getting too old for this."

Raylene added that she didn't think my uncle's heart could take much more stress. "He almost had a heart attack last night!"

She said she thought it might be best if they took me right then and there. "Maybe you could find her one of them religious boarding schools? The good Lord can work miracles if you let him."

So I picked up my black Hefty bag and dragged it down the stairs. They took me to the children's shelter in Lancaster where I would stay for about a week.

I tried not to cry when the caseworker led me away because I didn't want Uncle Melvin to know how much this was hurting me inside. He was sniffling into a white handkerchief, which he held in his big-knuckled hands.

But Raylene didn't shed a tear.

"Listen," she said smugly, "when the Lord gets you better, you can always come back here and live with us."

I felt like spitting in her face. This wasn't a matter of getting *better*, it was a matter of getting *somewhere*, and why she couldn't understand that still makes me crazy.

It was the week before Christmas and I was eleven years old.

P.S. Raylene had the nerve to ask Midge if I could visit them after I first came to Alison's last June, but I said no thanks. I was a ward of the courts now, and I had a choice. I might miss my Uncle Melvin, but I **never** want to see Raylene again.

November 26

Okay, I haven't written for over a week, but I'm going to skip ahead to what happened at lunch today. Cat had been asking lately if she could sit with us at Paige's table, like I'm in charge of who sits with who or something.

"Ronnie, if you're not going to sit with me anymore, I think you *owe* it to me to ask." Now I totally wish I hadn't told her about the stupid necklace. Is she going to hold it over my head for all eternity?

The cafeteria was noisy with the little sixth graders leaving as we came in. After the pink-haired cafeteria lady handed me my change, I saw Cat carrying her tray to the table where she sat alone every day (where I used to sit). She turned and looked directly at me, like *today was the day*, so I'd better get going or she would probably stare at me the whole entire lunch.

While Britnee and I were getting into our seats with our green salads and pizza on our trays, I said to Paige, "Can Cat sit at our table today? She wanted me to ask."

My question hung in the air between us, like in the movies when somebody lobs a hand grenade and you're waiting to see if it explodes. Paige flipped her brown hair over her shoulder, opened her horrified mouth, then shut it again.

(This is exactly why I didn't want to ask.)

"Not permanently," I explained, eyeing Sarika, who at times can be somewhat reasonable. I tried again. "Can't we ever be *nice*?"

Still no answer. But they all looked over in Cat's direction.

Cat was still standing by her table, in her tight beige top and two-sizes-too-small brown pleather pants. Sarika sniffed like there was a bad smell in the air. "No wonder nobody likes her," she said. "What's up with those pants?"

"She's always been fashion-challenged," said Britnee.

(Even I had to admit that was kind of funny.)

"Should I tell her to forget it—or what?" I wished really hard that we could forget the whole thing.

Unexpectedly, Paige grinned in a mischievous kind of way. "No, tell her to come over. Go get her, Ronnie. It might be fun."

What? How could anything *fun* come from this? I had a sinking feeling, but I went over to get her anyway and told her not to blow it, to follow my lead, to sit there and hardly say anything, and maybe (with any luck) they might even forget she was there.

Cat began to sit down right next to me, which of course I didn't want, so I made an excuse about having to sit on the other side. Then we began eating, or at least pushing food around on our plates.

Cat seemed kind of nervous but she took a big bite of her cheeseburger and when she did some ketchup plopped down from her chin to the table. "Do you want any of my fries, Ronnie?" she asked.

Britnee rolled her eyes.

I told her no thanks and handed her a napkin for her chin.

Britnee was the first to say something, like they had it all planned.

"Those pants, Cat. Did you get them at the mall?"

Cat was smiling, flattered they had noticed, I guess. "I got them at Sears," she answered proudly, her mouth full of food. "On sale. Right, Ronnie?"

She was smirking, like, *see, I told you they would let me in.*

I had a pit in the bottom of my stomach.

"Brown is the perfect color for you, *considering,*" said Britnee.

"Brown and white," said Sarika, and they started laughing at their inside joke.

Cat tried to catch my eye, like, *are they laughing at me?* Her poor round face was hurt and confused. I shrugged and didn't say a thing.

Paige announced that she was dying of thirst, and went to get a diet soda from the machine in back of the room. She rolled her short skirt up a notch before she walked past the popular boys, like Tyler and Jon, who were sitting at a nearby table.

When she returned, she popped open the can. "Hey, Cat?" she asked, taking a sip. "Maybe you can answer this. Speaking of the mall. Why didn't you meet us there two Saturdays ago?"

"Yeah," said Britnee, taking out a packet of mints. "We waited there for you—for like *hours.*"

Cat looked puzzled. She knew they hadn't asked her to go to the mall. She looked at me as if I could translate, but I just shook my head.

"You didn't ask me to go to the mall," she said

carefully.

"What?" said Paige, acting surprised. "We *told* Ronnie to invite you." Then she eyed me. "We told you to invite her, Ronnie. Didn't you want Cat to come?"

I have to admit, I didn't know what to say at this point because, of course, they didn't tell me to invite Cat or I would have. Cat was looking at me like I was the worst friend *ever*. I felt totally uncomfortable—and guilty—for something I didn't even do.

(Besides, you have to agree that this was a trick question. No matter how I answered I would be in trouble with someone.) I took a mouthful of salad so I didn't have to answer.

"Never mind," Paige said. "Maybe next time. We have something else much more important that we simply *must* tell you, Cat. Something about your *pants*."

That's when I knew it was going to get *really* bad.

"You've got to lose the pleather," said Paige. "No offense, but those pants make you look really *huge*. And your boobs look so big in that shirt. They're like udders, really."

"What?" Cat seemed bewildered, because one minute they were being nice to her and the next . . . well, it was like she was being ambushed.

"Simply *bovine*," said Britnee, nodding.

Paige's eyes swept over the table. "Ready guys?"

"*Moooooo!*" she yelled.

Everybody else began mooing, too, because that's the new thing we do when somebody looks fat. I just sat there frozen, but they looked at me like, *wasn't I going to* moo *with them*? So I turned my head and made a *moo* sound (barely audible, so I don't think Cat heard me).

I watched out of the corner of my eye as Cat's face

crumpled—like when you stomp on a soda can. She pushed her chair away from the table, stood up, and looked at me like, *wasn't I going to come with her? Wasn't I going to be on her side?*

She must have thought I was a much better friend. When she realized I wasn't, she turned abruptly and began walking fast.

Then, poor Cat, as she hurried out of the lunch-room, she knocked over somebody's tray. So of course everyone started clapping and cheering, because that's what we do when somebody drops their tray. She ran really fast after that.

It took a while for everyone to stop laughing at our table, but I felt like I was going to throw up. After things quieted down, Paige said, "Don't look so upset, Ronnie. *You* wanted her to sit with us." Then they all finished eating their salads, but none of them ate any pizza.

When I got home after school, Alison was still at her office. I tried to see if Cat was online so I could check how she was doing, because she had pretty much disap-peared after lunch. But her Away Message was on, so I called and said on her answering machine that I hoped she was doing okay.

Then I laid down on my soft denim comforter, my eyes fixed on the crack in my bedroom ceiling, and thought about what had happened in the lunchroom today. I felt like the worst hypocrite in the entire world. I hated myself! It wasn't right to treat people that way. I should know better. Plenty of kids had done stuff like that to me.

I felt this terrible pressure inside me, like I just had

to do something or I was going to explode. I couldn't
stand being in my own skin!

The next thing I knew, I found myself standing in
Alison's bedroom. I walked over to her antique oak
dresser, with the family photographs in silver frames
neatly arranged on either side of the mirror. My eyes
fixed on her square white leather jewelry box. Opening
the lid, I slowly moved aside a pair of Alison's silver hoop
earrings, her bulky college ring, and an old Timex watch.
Finally I found what I was looking for: a solid gold charm
bracelet that held about twenty different charms. My
favorite was a ballet shoe with two tiny diamonds (Alison
used to dance). I also liked the heart with a key.

So pretty!

As I held the tiny clasp between my fingers, the
charms made a tinkling noise like a wind chime. I let the
bracelet swing slowly back and forth in front of the oval
mirror, watching it glitter and shine. The afternoon sunlight bouncing off it created a series of dots on the wall
behind the bed; it was hypnotizing. Then, I got an idea.

Maybe . . . if I borrowed it for a while . . . Alison
would probably figure she'd lost it somewhere. I could
always put it back.

My heart was pumping and a nervous tingle ran
down my spine.

Should I take it? Or not?

Then I heard a noise outside. I had to make my
decision fast. Her car was pulling into the driveway!

My fist suddenly tightened around the bracelet so
hard that my fingernails bit into the palm of my hand. I
closed the lid of the box, and quickly backed away. Then
I pushed the bracelet into my pocket and ran out of her
room.

December 6

Red-felt Christmas stockings had been hanging on the bulletin board in the lobby outside Midge's office since the week before Thanksgiving. I pointed them out to Alison when we arrived for the annual holiday party for foster families on Saturday afternoon.

The names of the agency's foster children (who were available and waiting for adoption) were stenciled in gold glitter on the white tops of the stockings. My name was on one of them with a snapshot of me stapled underneath it. It was like an advertisement for lost pets you might see in the newspaper.

"Can you believe it?" I said to her. "Pathetic."

"I agree," said Alison as she gently rubbed my shoulders. "Couldn't they figure out something else?"

Midge stood near the fake Christmas tree in the corner of the lobby, wearing a green sweatshirt that said, "Ho! Ho! Ho!" She was handing out paper cups filled with red punch to a group of misbehaved little kids who clamored to open the presents that were stacked under the fake tree.

I didn't go near them. I had been to enough of these parties to know that most of the presents would be clothing items bought by well-meaning grown-ups who knew absolutely nothing about fashion. I asked Alison if we could leave soon, because I didn't need any more clothes, and I felt totally awkward being here, like I didn't belong. She said okay, and went to get a packet of papers she needed from Midge. Alison put the papers into her canvas bag, and then we snuck out the back.

It was a cold, dreary day. Big, fat raindrops hit the windshield occasionally, and we had to turn the heat on in the car. Alison decided that since we didn't stay at the party, we had time now to pick out our Christmas tree instead. As we drove to the tree farm, Alison told me that when she was a little girl, she went there every year with her family to pick out their tree. A horse-drawn wagon in the parking lot would take them into the forest where the trees were grown. When she and her parents decided on the perfect tree, her dad would chop it down. Afterward they would stay and listen to the carolers in the barn and drink hot apple cider, and her father would tell her how special and precious she was to them.

Alison's eyes misted at the memory. "I didn't have any siblings, Ronnie, just like you."

What was she talking about?

"Excuse me? Are you forgetting? I have two brothers."

She seemed flustered and apologized. "I'm sorry. What I meant was how you're living now . . . alone, here with me."

Alison said she didn't mind being an only child, except that when her parents got older and sick, the burden of taking care of them fell completely on her.

"It was so hard after my parents died," she said. "I don't have much family left. There's only my cousin in Philadelphia, and my great aunt in Florida. That was another reason I decided to take you in."

What? Was I supposed to take the place of her real family?

I wanted to tell her, *but I already have a family.* Except that my family didn't have any holiday traditions, unless you wanted to count Kenny getting drunk off his butt every Christmas, and my equally wasted mother ordering pizza so we could have something to eat.

But that was in the past. The last time we talked, my

mother sounded like she was making real progress.

"I've been clean for two whole weeks now," she said proudly.

"Does that mean you'll be sending for me soon?"

"Christ! What did I say about pressuring me?"

"Okay. I'm sorry. I just got excited, that's all."

I was glad for my brothers that she had stopped doing drugs, since they deserve to have her healthy and taking care of them. But I will never stop praying for all of us to be together as a family again one day, and I really hope Alison knows that by now.

The tree farm was just how Alison had described it, except that now instead of horses they used a red farm tractor to pull the wagon.

It was drizzling as we walked through the forest, and muddy leaves stuck to our shoes. We decided on a tree, a Fraser fir, and the man tied it onto the roof of our car. They were also selling miniature tabletop trees in the barn, and Alison let me pick one out for my room. That was so nice of her. Now we are going to have *two* trees!

(Some years with my mother we didn't even have *one*.)

As soon as we got home, I let Lucky outside to go to the bathroom and then I went upstairs to set up my tree. We needed an extension cord for the miniature lights. Alison managed to find one in the basement and brought it into my room. But while she was moving the lamp on my dresser to plug it in, something terrible happened.

I guess I didn't get a chance to put back the charm bracelet I had taken from her jewelry box. I'd meant to, after she'd mentioned it was missing the other day, but for some reason it had completely slipped my mind.

Her bracelet lay coiled there like a gold snake behind the lamp.

I quickly tried to scoop it up, but it was too late; Alison had already seen it. She grabbed it by the clasp and dangled it in front of me. Her face, reflected in the mirror of my bureau, first looked surprised, then exasperated, and then angry.

"Ronnie? What the *hell* is this doing here?"

She was going to be extremely upset about this, I could tell. I ran across the room and threw myself down on my bed, pulling the comforter over my head.

"Go away! I don't want to talk about it."

Alison tried to pull the covers off me, but I held on tight. "We're going to talk about it, right now, young lady! Whether you want to or not!"

She was practically screaming. "You swore to me you hadn't seen it! How could you sit there calmly watching TV when I spent the entire day looking for it? Turning the whole house upside down!"

I didn't say a thing.

"My father bought those charms for me. For my birthdays! On holidays! This bracelet is an important part of my past. It's all I have left of my family. You saw how distraught I was over losing it!"

What about *my* family, I was thinking. What did I have left of them?

But I still didn't say a word.

She took a deep breath. "How could you be so heartless?"

Heartless. Without a heart.

Didn't she know by now that I was evil?

About fifteen minutes later, Alison came back into my room. She sat down on the edge of my bed. "I'm sorry I got so angry before."

Her voice sounded calmer. "I would have gladly let you wear it if only you'd asked. But you *lied* about taking it—to my face. That's why I'm so upset. I thought I could trust you. Tell me, why did you take it in the first place?"

I held the pillow over my ears.

Why *had* I taken her charm bracelet?

To fill me up? To numb me? To stop the pain?

And why had I lied about it when she'd asked me?

Maybe I was embarrassed.

Or maybe, like in the past, I was afraid of what the punishment might be.

Alison put her hand on my shoulder. "I thought you were making progress," she said. "This is really a step back."

My voice was muffled. "I said I was sorry, what more do you want?"

"You *didn't* say you were sorry."

Why was she taking it so personally?

Couldn't she understand how this didn't have anything to do with her—and how it had everything to do with *me*?

Silence.

She was waiting for me to apologize, but for some reason the words refused to come.

"Maybe I should just call Midge," she said finally.

Was she thinking about sending me back? I came out from under my pillow. "You said no more violence! That we could *work* on the goddamn stealing!"

Alison's mouth was set in a line. "This isn't only about the stealing. You need to start taking ownership

72

for your behavior. After all these months you still don't seem to care much about *my* feelings. I know that life hasn't treated you fairly, but sometimes I wonder if you'll ever *truly* care about anyone but yourself."

With that, she got up from my bed and left the room.

Was she right about me not caring? What if I didn't know how?

I said a quick prayer.

Oh, please, dear God. I could show her if she would only give me . . .

One.

More.

Chance.

But was it too late?

Was she already calling Midge?

I raced out of my room and then paused at the top of the stairs. I guessed it wasn't too late—not yet—because there she was sitting below me on the bottom step. I could see her long gray hair, like a soft poncho, falling in a V shape over her shoulders. Her head was in her hands like she might be crying. I walked down the stairs and sat on the step behind her, my knees against her back.

"Please, Alison. Can you help me stop?"

What I really meant was, could she please help me stop wrecking every good thing that came my way? "I'm really, truly sorry. I care about you. Please, don't send me away."

She turned around, wiped away a tear, and stared right into my eyes. "I can't continue to invest all this time, all this energy . . . if you're not going to meet me halfway."

I nodded. "Okay, I will. I promise. I'll try. But you

don't understand what it's been like all these years—
having to depend on only myself."

Her face relaxed and she put a hand on my knee.
"That must have been awful. But, dear, you're not alone
anymore. You have *me* now. And your friends, and
Midge, and I bet even Francis would help you, if you'd
ask him."

She made it sound so easy, like there were all these
people just sitting around waiting for something to do.
I wanted to believe her, I really did, but I wasn't sure
there was anybody out there who could help somebody
who was as screwed up and evil . . . and *heartless* as me.

December 8

When I finally got in touch with Cat online, after the
lunchroom "incident," she seemed upset at first, but then
she got over it just as fast.

purrfect: y didn't u stand up for me, ronnie? that was
pretty low

heartrampled: i said i was sorry

purrfect: you did?

heartrampled: i can't control what they do

purrfect: its ok. i don't want to sit with them anymore. im just glad we can still be friends. we're still
friends, right?

heartrampled: right. gtg. cu

I hurried offline before she could ask me anything
else.

What I want to know is how she could "turn the
other cheek" so easily?

Whenever someone hurt me, I would go over and over it in my mind, like an angry scab, picking at it until it was raw and bleeding. Like yesterday, after my mother's phone call.

"*So what do you want for Christmas this year, Ronnie? A book? A CD?*"

"*You know what I really want.*"

"*No I don't.*"

"*When do you think I can come up there, Mom?*"

"*That again? I have to get a bigger apartment. Three bedrooms. That's what they told me. Which is expensive, which means another job, which you don't understand, Ronnie, I'm working full-time waitressing as it is.*"

"*So how much longer, Mom?*"

"*Plus no more drugs—not even pot—not even once in a while to help calm me down. They expect a whole lot, Veronica. It would take a whole lot to get you back. I'm just not sure I'm up to it. I have my own issues. It hasn't been easy, you know, leaving you behind.*"

What! It hasn't been easy for *her*?!

She got me so mad that I actually threw the phone when we were done!

But I can't ever picture Cat getting that angry. Whenever I did something really terrible to her, she made like it was no big deal, saying something like, *oh, well, try not to do it again.*

Sorry. Sorry. Sorry.

As forgiving as Cat was, this wasn't ever how it worked with Paige.

I first realized that something was wrong when

they weren't waiting by the lockers after fourth period. Paige and the rest of us always meet there then go to the bathroom before math. It was strange. They weren't absent; I'd seen them in homeroom. Somehow I must have just missed them.

I hurried up the stairs and into the bathroom and there they were, like usual (except without me): Britnee, Sarika, another girl named Jennafer, and in the middle of them was Paige. She was tying a pale blue bandanna around her head. "Do you think this matches my sweater?"

"Hey," I said, like normal, like they hadn't just tried to ditch me.

Paige didn't say anything and simply **pretended I wasn't there**. Britnee and Sarika did the same thing. No one said hello.

What the—?

"Hello? Guys?" I tried again, because maybe they hadn't heard me. "Is anything wrong? Why didn't you wait for me?"

All of the girls looked at Paige.

"Do you hear anybody talking?" said Paige, smiling, as she looked right through me. "I don't. Come on, we don't want to be late for class."

Then they laughed and walked out of the bathroom together, arm in arm, leaving me . . . standing all alone . . . at the sink.

I immediately panicked, and this big ball of sickness formed in my stomach. I couldn't picture myself going into math class or spending the rest of the day (or the rest of my life) with them ignoring me.

It was unbelievable. What had I done wrong?

Why were they doing this? I couldn't even stand the thought of going to class now.

I peered out the door, wanting to make sure that everyone had finished with their lockers and was safely in class. When I was sure the coast was clear, I casually walked down the empty hallway. Before I knew it, I stood directly in front of the small glass box of the fire alarm. As my heart pounded, I opened the door, quickly pulled down the bright red handle . . . and kept right on walking.

Blat! Ring. Blat! Ring. Blat! Ring.

It was incredible how quickly everybody emptied out of the classrooms. I managed to catch up with the tail end of my math class before they even realized I'd been missing. A weird calmness came over me and I now had some time to think.

I figured whatever I did wrong, I must have done it recently.

But what was it?

As I followed the crowd down the back stairwell to exit the school, I suddenly figured it out. The lunch-room! That had to be it! Paige must still be angry because I'd asked if Cat could sit with us at our table. This was her way of punishing me, of keeping me in line. But obviously I wasn't planning on doing anything that stupid ever again. I had to get her alone somehow . . . and explain.

Paige was huddled outside in the cold with Britnee and Sarika and a group of the popular boys, including Tyler Miller. Tyler had thick, dark eyebrows and curly brown hair. He was one of the tallest boys in eighth grade and his shoulders were very wide—he had even started to shave! Everyone thought he was so great, especially Paige. But last week when I'd been partners with him in science class, he kept trying to guess my bra size.

(Cat said he was so hot, and I should feel flattered 'cause it meant I was getting boobs.)

I went over to their group and stood directly behind Paige. Her long hair hung down the back of her blue sweater like a curtain separating me from the rest of them. I bumped my way into the circle, next to her and Tyler.

"It's freezing out!" said Britnee, rubbing her arms; none of us were wearing coats.

"Somebody pulled the alarm," Tyler said, smiling. "Know who did it, Ronnie?"

Paige gave him a dirty look just for asking.

"No," I replied, "but at least it got us out of class."

"Works for me," he said, grinning.

"Into the goddamn cold," snapped Paige.

I pulled gently at her sleeve. "Hey, could I talk to you for a minute? Alone? It's really important. *Please?*"

She shook her head. "I don't *think* so."

"Come on, *Pagers*," said Tyler, laughing. "We know you can be nice."

She turned around to face me, looking annoyed.

"Fine, Ronnie. But this better be worth it."

We walked toward the tennis courts as the fire truck drove into the parking lot. I only had a few minutes before they'd discover there was no fire, so I started talking fast.

"Cat isn't my friend anymore, not really. So if that's why you're ignoring me . . . because of the lunch thing . . ."

"What are you talking about?" she replied. "Didn't

Britnee tell you? You've turned into the biggest flirt.
Everyone knows you've started to think you're *all that.*"

"What?"

Was she crazy?

Paige stared at me with narrowed turquoise eyes,
until her gaze fell (for a quick second) on my tight-knit
sweater. Then she glanced nervously over at Tyler.

Suddenly, I got it. For some reason, she had begun
to see me as a threat.

"You're probably right," I said, thinking fast. "I'm
just missing Ross, that's all. Please don't be mad. I
didn't mean to act stuck-up. You guys are like *my whole
entire life!*"

"*Ross?*" Her eyes squinted like she didn't believe
me.

"Didn't I tell you? He's my boyfriend, from my
other school. Well, anyway, you and Tyler make a really
cute couple."

She smiled and looked over her shoulder again.
"You *think?*"

"Oh, *definitely.* He'd be crazy not to like you."

None of that boyfriend stuff was true, obviously, but
it totally seemed to work. Paige flipped back her hair
and tilted her head toward me. She was halfway to
being my friend again, I could tell. The teachers began
to call us to line up to go inside. We walked together
toward the line of kids heading into the building, until
she paused for a second right before we caught up to
them.

"Ronnie? I just thought of something. Did you pull
the fire alarm? Just so you could talk to me?"

I smiled shyly. "Would it matter?"

She grinned and took my hand in hers. "*Very* cool."

December 10

What I want to know is why do I keep doing things that I know deep down are wrong in the first place? Like lying and stealing, and pulling fire alarms, and throwing phones, and not sticking up for Cat?

I asked Francis when I saw him this morning what he thought my problem was, why my mother didn't want me, why I couldn't seem to stay in one place for very long, why my life was so incredibly messed up.

He told me to *wait right there*, while he walked the choir director out to her car. A wet snow had fallen the day before and the church smelled woodsy, like a cedar closet. Most of the parishioners had left or had gone to have a snack in the coffee area. I waited for him in a pew.

"Where's Alison?" Francis asked. He sat down beside me in his dress shirt and tie and shiny brown shoes, and glanced toward the big wooden doors at the back of the church. Sometimes he tried to chat with Alison when she would come get me after services (almost every Sunday since Francis had come back into my life).

"Grocery shopping. She said she might be a little late."

"Good. We have time. So tell me, what's going on?"

"The other day I threw a phone after talking to my mom."

"Really?" He looked surprised. "What was *that* all about?"

"I was in Midge's office right before our usual phone call. Midge was telling me that I needed to face reality, that my mother might *never* be ready for me. I got angry and said that wasn't true. So Midge said, okay, well, why don't you get on the phone and try to pin her down?"

"You've been waiting for your mom since I've known you," Francis said, in a way that was supportive and nice.

I shook my head. "It's true. Does she want me to keep measuring out my life in foster placements?"

Francis looked sad. He picked up a discarded church bulletin and put it into his jacket pocket and brushed some lint from his pants.

"My mother really didn't have a good answer."

"I'm so sorry," he said.

I sat in the pew, getting angry all over again, and told him about our conversation. He listened quietly without interrupting.

When I was finished, he let out a big sigh. "She said it wasn't easy leaving you behind?"

I pounded my hand on the pew. "How freaking easy does she think it's been for me?"

Francis put his hand on top of mine. "So what did you say after that?"

"Screw you."

"Pardon me?" He raised his eyebrows and glanced at me sideways.

"That's what I told her."

"Oh." He almost smiled. "You said 'screw you' to your mother?"

I nodded. "And that's when I threw the phone."

What I didn't tell him is how much I hate her sometimes. How I imagine myself going up there to her stupid, not-big-enough apartment and punching her in her lazy pot-smoking face—until she's black-and-blue and begging for mercy. I hate her so much for putting me through this. For not caring enough to even try.

I glanced behind the minister's pulpit. The figure of Jesus on the cross was hanging over the altar with his hands held open—palms up, nail-holes exposed.

"Do you believe God sends people to hell for their sins?" I asked.

Francis shook his head. "You're thinking some very deep thoughts this morning."

"I'm not a nice person. You'd be wondering about that too, if you were me."

"Everyone has a dark side, Ronnie," he said softly. "But God loves the whole of us, even our bad parts."

"That's easy for you to say. God would never send you to hell."

But then Francis surprised me by telling me something about his past. "You don't know this, Ronnie," he explained, "but after my wife, Barbara, died from breast cancer, I completely fell apart. I was so very, very angry! Why did she have to leave me? Why hadn't God answered my prayers? I began drinking heavily. I even stopped going to church."

"You did *what*?"

"I was feeling sorry for myself."

"Oh."

"Then a lady friend of Barbara's began trying to help me, but I was still nasty. When she knocked on my door, I told her to go away. I said she was interfering. But she pushed her way in and put up with my raging, until she finally said to me, 'God isn't here to stop bad things from happening, but to help us deal with them when they do.'

"After that she signed me up as a volunteer for the youth group—without my consent. Boy, was I ever mad at her then! But I went anyway. I don't know why. Maybe deep down I knew it would help. And gradually, caring about the kids in youth group did help me. And a while later, around the time you and I met, I was pretty much content most of the time. I think God waited for me, because he loved me, even when I was being a jerk."

"But you suffered. Your wife died. You had a reason to be upset. Some of the things I've done—"

"Think about how much you love Lucky," he said, interrupting, "even when he does bad things. It's exactly the same."

I admit that I did love Lucky even after he stole my last piece of stuffed-crust pizza, the one that I'd left on the coffee table. And I loved him when he chewed a hole in my new sneaker—okay, that's not totally true, but I only stopped loving him for about five whole minutes. So I understand what Francis means about being able to love someone when they do something wrong.

But dogs are innocent, especially puppies. Lucky doesn't mean to do the bad things he does; it's not *intentional*—he just can't help himself.

I'm not so sure about God loving me, because . . . well . . . I guess I *do* mean to do at least half the things I do wrong. It *is* intentional.

And speaking of bad things, I'm not sure if I still love my mother. Not if she's not up to even *trying* to get me back. Doesn't she think I'm worth it? And if I don't love her, what does that say about me?

"God loves us, even the bad parts," Francis repeated.

But I wondered, how in the world could that be?

Christmas Day—December 25

Alison told me that she'd been awake for hours. She'd put on a pot of coffee, baked my favorite cinnamon sticky buns, and read all of the newspaper—every section—even the boring sports pages.

"Hi," I said, yawning as I came down the stairs. It was almost ten thirty. My hair was hanging wet from my shower and I'd pushed it behind my ears. I was wearing a T-shirt and gray sweatpants, which were the most comfortable clothes I had.

"I've been waiting for you!" said Alison, dressed in fancy black pants and a holiday sweater. "How could you sleep so late—on *Christmas*?"

She seemed upset with me, disappointed.

"Excuse me, but at our house my mother *never* got up before noon!"

Alison's face fell. "I'm so sorry. I wasn't thinking. Are you missing your . . . ?" she paused. "Holidays must be extra hard for you, dear."

Could that have been it? Was I missing my family? I'd woken up with a headache and taken awfully long in the shower. In fact, I'd almost gone back to bed.

Alison brought me a sticky bun on a plate with snowflakes around the edges. "Here, have something to eat. I won't push. I understand. That first Christmas after my parents died, I felt the very same way."

Was she serious? She'd never felt the same way as me!

"My mother isn't dead, Alison."

Besides, now that she'd forced me to think about it, it wasn't my mother's absence I was upset about, not really. It was that Christmas, in general, had never been fun for me. It was exactly two years ago that my uncle and Raylene had dumped me into foster care. I didn't want to think about that time of my life, how abandoned I felt, how betrayed. But Alison could see the pain very much alive on my face.

"Of course not," she said sadly. "I only meant . . . " She paused. "I just wanted to make this, our first Christmas together, extra special."

Now that I was fully awake, I scanned the room. Everything *did* look special. She'd put on holiday music, the tree was lit, and that wonderful-smelling cinnamon bun was waiting for me next to a steaming mug of hot chocolate.

"Let's not fight," she pleaded. "It's *Christmas*."

I looked at the mantel where the empty stockings we'd hung last night were now bulging with all sorts of surprises.

"Okay. But can Lucky open his stocking first?"

Alison took down his stocking and put it on the floor. Lucky didn't dart away from it like he usually does with something new. He immediately sniffed out a treat and then completely devoured it with a loud crunching sound that made us laugh.

He played with his next present, which was a stuffed animal I had bought for him at the mall. He tossed the fuzzy sheep toy up into the air several times. After he got tired of doing that, he settled onto his beanbag bed, holding the toy protectively between his front paws, as if daring us to take it. He was the cutest dog *ever*.

Alison handed me my stocking next. Inside were a dozen packages neatly wrapped in gold foil paper and tied with a string. She'd bought me my favorite hygiene products: bath salts, a ChapStick, a package of breath mints, some new lip gloss, and a toothbrush.

I gathered my new things, and began to walk toward the stairs. "Well, thanks for everything," I said.

"Wait!" she said quickly. "Don't you want to open anything else?"

I hung my head and stared at the floor.

Did I mention the huge pile of gifts around the tree? There were more gifts under there than I'd seen in my entire life!

"Ronnie, what's wrong?"

"It's just that . . . there are so *many* presents."

Alison nodded, smiling broadly. "And they're all for you."

I anxiously chewed on a fingernail. I felt . . . *over-whelmed.*

"Don't you want to see what I got you?" she asked.

What was I supposed to say? That I didn't deserve all these gifts? That nobody had ever treated me like this before?

"Ronnie?"

"It's just that my mom usually gets me something small. Like a shirt or something; a book or a CD. And when I was in the other foster homes, most of the stuff went to the *real* kids in the family, you know, *not* me."

She was watching me closely, like, *so?*

"Alison, I only got you *one* present."

"Oh?"

"Remember that forty dollars you gave me to spend on gifts at the mall? By the time I got something for Paige and Britnee . . . and Lucky's toy . . . and Francis's present, there wasn't much left over for anyone else."

Not even Cat, I suddenly remembered. "Honestly, I just didn't know."

Alison shook her head. "Nobody's keeping count, silly. It doesn't matter what you spent on me, okay? There were so many things you needed. Let me spoil you. Just open one at a time. And if you don't like something, we can always take it back."

"Okay," I said, relieved. "But let me go get yours first."

I ran upstairs and came back with her present. "Here. I hope you like it. Merry Christmas."

I peered over her shoulder as Alison unwrapped my gift. It was a self-help book. She read the title aloud. "*Foster Parenting 101. Helping Your Attachment-Disordered Child Without Losing Your Mind.*"

She laughed. "So you think I'm losing my mind, huh?"

"No! That's not why I got it for you," I explained. "The lady at the store said . . . I just thought . . . it might help . . . you know . . . with *me*."

"How thoughtful," she said, smiling. Then she paused. "But I want you to know that I don't believe in labels. You're worth much more than that. I'm so happy you're here with me this Christmas."

I replied, "Sure, I know," like *of course*, but actually I was filled with these warm and special feelings.

"Okay, now," she said. "Let's get you started."

She handed me my gifts one by one. It took nearly an hour for me to open them all. There was an oversized sweatshirt from Old Navy, and a fleece bathrobe, a few pairs of earrings, slippers with dog faces on the toe part, a new CD player(!) because I had dropped my old one, and lots more. I thought I was finally finished, but she'd saved the biggest presents for last.

She placed two huge boxes in front of me. "I can't wait for you to open these!"

I peeled off the large sheets of gold wrapping paper, and pulled two suitcases—an overnight shoulder bag and a weekender bag (with wheels)—out of the over-sized boxes. They were maroon, with a tapestry fabric, trimmed in tan leather. When I put the larger piece of luggage on the floor and unzipped it, Lucky jumped right in!

"Lucky, no!" Alison clapped her hands. "Aren't they neat? Don't you just love them?"

"Am I going somewhere?" I asked, getting nervous.

"No, silly. I mean, sure, someday. We'll go on lots of trips together. For now, why not use them for sleep-overs? I've noticed how you just stuff your things into your pillowcase. That's not very organized, is it? See how this one has compartments? You could put your blow dryer in here and then . . ."

I wasn't saying anything.

Alison stopped. "What's wrong now? You look upset."

"Nobody uses suitcases for sleepovers."

"They don't?"

I shook my head. "Very geeklike."

"Okay. Well, at least we can finally get rid of that black garbage bag up in your room. I mean, Ronnie, it's more like three bags, with all of your things stuffed inside, and it looks so *temporary*, like you're going to race out of here any minute and . . ."

I fiddled with the zipper on the shoulder bag, not meeting her eyes.

"Don't you like the color?" she said.

How was I going to explain this?

"No, I like them . . . they're nice. Thanks. But, I'm not

getting rid of the bag in my room. It's the original. The one I packed the day my mother left me. I *need* to keep it around. I don't know why exactly, except . . . it's like a good luck charm or something."

"Oh," she said sadly. "I see."

But I could tell she didn't.

"Look, if I get rid of it now, it would mean my mom's never coming back for me, like I've given up hope! And I haven't, not completely, anyway. Besides, like I told Midge, if I start using a suitcase, it means I have a real home to go back *to*—"

"But *this* is your home!"

"No, it isn't! You're just getting me ready for somewhere else."

Alison placed her coffee cup on the table.

I shrugged. "Right?"

"Ronnie?" she said tenderly. "Look at me. I realize that you're devoted to your mother and that you want more than anything to be with her someday. I hope it works out for you, truly, I do. But if it doesn't . . . work out with her, I mean . . . I was hoping . . . What I'm trying to say is . . . I've decided I want to file . . . for adoption."

What?

I was totally shocked. "You want to adopt *me*?"

Alison laughed. "Is that so surprising?"

"Don't you realize that I've never stayed *anywhere* this long? Outside of my uncle's, that is—because something *always* goes wrong. What if something goes wrong?"

I stood up so fast that I got all dizzy and suddenly I had a pounding headache.

It felt like my head was one of those lottery machines you see on TV after the six o'clock news. It was as if all the parts of my life—all the places I'd been, all the people who had taken care of me (or had *not* taken care of me)—were like those numbered balls inside a lottery machine, bouncing off one another in my mind.

(At least on TV if they came bouncing out in exactly the right order, you could win the lottery! But I'd never had that kind of luck.)

"I don't know about this," I said, starting to panic. "Have you thought about this? I'm not a very good person, Alison. I lie. I steal stuff, remember? Do you realize what you're getting into?"

Lucky followed behind me as I paced across the room. Then he started to whine.

Alison stood up, put her hands on my shoulders to stop me, and looked directly into my eyes. "I know *exactly* what I'm getting into. I'm positive. I'm sure. You may find this hard to believe . . ." Alison cleared her throat, hesitating. "But I guess I've sort of grown . . . to *love* you."

I gulped back a tear.

"There, I've said it." She smiled. "There's no turning back now."

I must have looked stunned. My bottom lip quivered. I didn't know whether to burst out sobbing from disbelief or run out of the room in pure terror.

I forced myself to look at her face. Alison's eyes were the most beautiful that I'd ever seen them. "Come here, sweetheart," she said, pulling me into her arms.

She gave me a hug, a long and meaningful hug, a hug that clearly marked for both of us a different path—one that we would travel together. I held on to her so tightly that it must have hurt. Her shoulder quickly became damp with my silent tears. I noticed with a start that I was trembling; but it didn't matter because Alison was too.

Part Two
Obliterated

New Year's Eve—December 31

Today was Alison's birthday. We went to the movies and then came home and ordered pizza. We put nine candles in the middle of the pizza (because we didn't have forty-five), and I sang "Happy Birthday." Then I gave her a card that I'd made that she said was better than any store-bought card she'd ever received. It was my best New Year's Eve ever, coming right after my best Christmas in a long time, so what could happen to spoil it?

Cat, that's what.

After we got home from the movies, Cat invited her-self for a sleepover because her mom had gone to see Bud's band play at some bar.

"Please, Ronnie? I don't want to be alone."

When she got here we had some birthday cake from Redner's and a bowl of popcorn. We sat together on the couch and watched the ball drop on MTV. Cat and I decided to go upstairs right after Alison did, so we wouldn't regret falling asleep on the cold, hard floor. We were listening to music (quietly) and getting ready for bed.

I put on my new bathrobe from Alison—which I love because it's navy blue fleece with gold stars and moons on the sleeves. Cat changed into the T-shirt she slept in, and that's when I noticed the cut marks on her arms . . . and things got kind of weird.

Red horizontal scratches crisscrossed the top of her left arm. Some cuts were scabbed over and others were faded white scars. I grabbed at her sleeve before she could pull it away. "What the *hell* is that?"

"It's no big deal. Sometimes I cut myself."

I'd heard about girls who cut themselves. It looked like a big deal to me.

"And you do that *because* . . . ?"

"I don't know. It's kind of fun."

I gave her a look like, *you can't be serious.*

"Okay, it helps me feel better. I'm under a lot of stress."

"You are? What stress?"

Cat burst into tears then, and her voice became all high-pitched and whiny. Mascara dripped like spiderwebs down her face.

"Please tell me what's wrong," I asked her like a hundred times, but she couldn't stop crying. "Is it something I did? Or Paige?"

"NO!" she sobbed, and cried even harder.

Feeling really worried, I took her chubby hands in mine and held them in what I hoped was a comforting way. While I was waiting for her to calm down, I stared at the silver rings she wore on every finger: one had a pair of hearts intertwined; another was in the shape of a dragon.

Finally she stopped crying, pushed back her black choppy hair, and blew her nose. "It's Bud," she said, sniffling. "When Mom's working and I'm home alone with him. He hangs around outside my door when I'm changing my clothes. He opens the door really quietly so I don't even hear him!"

I remembered how he stared at us in the pool.

"Oh my God! That is soooo creepy."

She nodded. "And last week when I was walking past the couch, I felt his fingers brush against my butt. He made some lame excuse like I had crumbs on my pants."

I shuddered in disgust. "What is he, like a pervert or something?"

She shrugged. "I'm scared, Ronnie." Her eyes welled up. Another tear slipped down her face, onto her lips, and disappeared. "What if he tries something worse?"

"You should tell your mom. She should definitely know about this."

"I can't." Cat shook her head. "He'd only deny it. Besides, she probably wouldn't believe me anyway. Whenever I tell her about anything he does, I get grounded for telling lies about *him*."

I pictured Cat's mom, Karen, with her tight jeans and short black hair spiked with gel. She never seemed particularly happy, even if she'd always been nice to me.

"Don't tell anyone, Ronnie. Promise? I don't want my mom to get mad. Without Bud's paycheck we can't make the rent on our house."

Cat swore she'd let me know if things got out of control, so I said okay, even though if you ask me, they already sounded out of control. After she calmed down, I told her about Alison and maybe being adopted. "She wants me to think about it, and let her know if I want her to file."

"That's great!" Cat said, smiling widely. "We'll be so awesome together in high school! I was afraid you'd have to move again."

"I guess. But honestly, I still want to be with my real family. I miss them so much." I took the picture of my mom and brothers out of my bag and handed it to her. "Alison's nice, don't get me wrong, but it's just not the same."

"I see the resemblance," Cat said, studying the picture. "You should definitely go up there, if that's what you want. I'd give anything to get out of this place."

I gave her a look like, *are you kidding me?*

"I can't just *go* up there, Cat. I have to wait. Until

everyone says that my mom is ready and off drugs and in a new apartment—which she isn't. Not yet. Who knows, maybe she won't ever be ready for me—and Alison wants me *now*."

"Good things are worth waiting for," she replied.

Cat was right, of course, about good things being worth the wait. But I didn't tell her that a small part of me was beginning to wonder if my mom had *ever* been what you'd call a "good thing."

New Year's Day—January 1

Today Alison planned to take me to Allentown for a New Year's Day celebration that she thought might be "culturally stimulating." I've learned that this is her code phrase for "this is going to bore the crap out of you," so I wasn't exactly looking forward to it.

As I waited for her to finish getting ready (hoping she would take a long time), there was a knock on our door, which was surprising because I knew we weren't expecting anybody. When I opened the door, a familiar-looking man wearing funky black leather pants, a big leather jacket, and mirrored sunglasses that wrapped around his whole face was standing on our stoop.

"Francis?" He'd never come to our house before.

He took off his sunglasses and smiled. "Do you want to go for a *ride?*"

"Huh?"

He pointed to the street. Parked in front of our house was this huge motorcycle with a sidecar! The motorcycle was shiny black with a silver engine and gigantic wheels. All curves and metal. The sidecar attached at the base was half the size of the motorcycle and looked like a bumper car you might see at Funland.

"I got myself a Christmas present," he said.

"Oh my God," I screamed. "It's *awesome!*"

"It's called a Gold Wing. I got the sidecar so I can bring Checkers along sometimes," he explained. He smiled again, looking proud. "Go sit on it, if you'd like."

I ran out into the street without even first putting on my shoes, and jumped onto the big leather seat. The handlebars felt cold on my hands, but something about sitting there made me feel warm and wild, with no limits on where I could go.

Alison came outside a few minutes later, closing the door behind her.

I waved to her from my perch on the bike. "Francis is taking me for a ride!"

"If that's okay with you," he added quickly.

I saw Alison shake her head no and heard her say something like she was very sorry but I couldn't possibly go with him since we already had plans—First Day in Allentown—but thanks just the same.

What? She was going to ruin everything!

I hopped off the motorcycle and ran to the door.

Alison wasn't smiling. "I wish you would have called first, Francis. We need to leave right now or we'll be late."

He seemed awfully disappointed, but then his eyes twinkled at me. "I have an idea. I'm free the whole afternoon. What if I took you there?" he offered. "Both of you? On the bike? It's perfectly safe. I've been riding for more than ten years."

"*Please,*" I begged. "We *never* do anything fun."

Alison looked from Francis to me and back again. "I think I'm outnumbered here," she said, laughing.

"You don't happen to have three helmets with you?"

Francis grinned sheepishly. "As a matter of fact, I do."

Alison went upstairs to change into warmer clothes, because even though it was forty-nine degrees outside (a record!), it could still get pretty cold on a motorcycle on the first day of January. I put on my new ski jacket and was warm and cozy with one of Francis's wool blankets wrapped around me in my very own private sidecar.

It was the most incredible experience I've ever had. It was like flying! No wonder they called it a Gold "Wing." Everything looked clearer and more real without a car window getting in the way. When we stopped at a stop sign heading out of town, I could see myself in the shiny chrome of the wheel cover. (I have to admit I looked very cool!)

On the back roads to Allentown, all of the farm stands were closed for the winter, but you could see the faded signs leaning against old wooden barns that said "Quilts 4 Sale." The surrounding hills were mostly brown dirt and tan grasses with melting snow mixed in, and long fat shadows when the sun peeked out from behind the clouds. I counted five hawks circling high above us over the fields. It was beautiful.

Alison wrapped her arms around Francis's waist. When we stopped at traffic lights she glanced over to check on me with this excitement in her eyes, like, *can you believe we're doing this?* Every now and then Francis would turn around, smile, and give me a thumbs-up sign, which I had to return before he would start riding again.

(Corny, I know, but that's Francis.)

Alison had told me when I'd first moved in that

she'd given up on dating men. She said divorcing twice was bad enough, but who would come see a therapist who'd been divorced three times? "I'm terribly unlucky in love," she'd explained.

Yet now, seeing her so relaxed and happy with Francis, I wondered if she was beginning to change her mind.

First Day wasn't nearly as boring as I'd thought it might be. We went to a comedy improv show—very funny! We also saw dancers with masks from Thailand, a magician on a unicycle, and some gospel singers. I wanted to stay longer, but Francis said it would be too cold to ride on the motorcycle if we waited long past dark.

On the way back we stopped at a Schatz's Diner for something to eat, which was one of those diners that looked sort of like a silver-colored trailer at the side of the road. Alison ate a Reuben sandwich and I had a chicken Caesar salad. Through the windows of the diner we saw people stop and stare at Francis's incredible motorcycle in the parking lot. I imagined they were saying things like, "Whose awesome motorcycle is this?"

(I was pretending it was mine.)

While we were eating dessert—chocolate pudding pie with whipped cream—Francis asked me about my New Year's resolution, which we'd talked about in youth group the week before. "So Ronnie, what did you decide?"

"That's easy. I'm not going to lie anymore."

Both he and Alison raised their eyebrows and gave each other a look that got me kind of upset.

"What's the matter?" I cried. "Don't you believe me?"

Alison was wearing her gold charm bracelet. She

quietly readjusted the clasp. "I'm sorry. I just assumed you would say you didn't want to *steal* anymore."

"No, I'm all set with that."

"Oh?" she said, looking surprised.

"Yes. It's been almost a month now."

"Still," Francis said, "it's hard to stop doing something, *anything*, once it's become a habit."

"Maybe for some people," I said, taking another scoop of my pie.

They didn't seem exactly convinced, but that's okay, I don't blame them. They didn't realize that the stealing was connected to the lying, and that for me, a lie was whenever I found myself doing something I didn't believe in—or when I didn't trust the truth of my heart.

Like if I told myself that doing bad things was the only way I could deal with my problems, then that was a lie, because I was actually capable of choosing other ways to deal. And if I thought I had to do whatever it took to be popular, then that was a lie, too, because I **so** didn't have to do that either.

Just when I had it all figured out, Alison had to bring up something else. "Remember, Ronnie, not telling the whole truth is also lying."

"Lying by omission," Francis agreed.

I thought about the percentage of things I left out whenever I told them *anything*. After a few minutes I said, "Look, obviously I'm going to work on the lying *and* the stealing. But I think if I just listen to my heart, it will tell me the right thing to do."

Francis grinned. "That sounds perfect."

Alison looked skeptical, but she managed a smile. Francis paid for our dinners as a special treat, then we strapped on our helmets and went outside.

It was dark on the highway, the temperature had dropped, and the wind felt cold and biting on my face. Honestly, I was starting to wish we had taken the car. But as we cruised down the farm-lined roads of Route 222, it was so clear and crisp out that I could see Orion's belt with its three bright stars in the winter sky over the hillside.

(That's my favorite constellation.)

As we rode past some of the farmhouses with their lights flickering through the trees like candles, it was surprisingly easy to imagine living a normal life with a real family, with people who would love you exactly the way you are.

When we roared back into Liberty, I was pretty cold, but it was worth every degree of coldness, I decided. The day had been so awesome!

Later that night, I snuggled into my bed, pulling my denim comforter over my head, but I still had trouble falling asleep. I tossed and turned. What was I so worried about?

Being adopted, of course. Nobody has ever treated me as nice as Alison (except my mom . . . sometimes), but adoption means FOREVER.

Was I completely ready?

Alison tries to make it seem like she isn't pressuring me, but I can tell she wants me to make up my mind. Yet how can I without hurting someone? Seriously, how would my mother feel if I didn't wait for her? She might hate me! And what about my brothers? If I was adopted, could I ever see them again? And what would it mean if I said no to Alison? Would she send me back into temporary foster care?

I turned on my light and took out the picture of

my family and had a silent conversation with them in my mind. "I don't want to hurt anyone's feelings," I told them, "but how would you feel if I stayed?"

I breathed quietly to hear what my heart might be saying.

Unfortunately, it wasn't saying a thing.

With such a huge decision facing me, the future seems suddenly scary and unsure.

I just wish that I could stay **right here** in **this night** at the beginning of a new year, when everything seems like a clean slate, when I don't have to decide about lying or telling the truth, or listening to my heart and hoping it tells me the right thing to do. I wish I could just ride along in that safe and cozy sidecar forever—and let somebody else be in charge of watching out for all the danger.

January 14

Tonight the three of us (Paige, Britnee, and I) went ice-skating at Red Bridge Pond near the high school. Paige was wearing a new pale pink ski jacket, which looked perfect with her long dark hair. It was so cold outside that I could see my breath—white fog in the freezing air. Earlier this afternoon, we'd noticed some boys shoveling a thin layer of snow off the pond to play ice hockey, and that was when Paige decided we should go skating later.

It was dark as we walked down the hill. The round skating area was lit by bright floodlights, but this pond was long and went on for about a quarter of a mile. The teenagers skated at the narrow end, under the rusty red bridge near the bonfire.

The round part of the pond was crowded with lots of little kids and families. We sat down on an old log to put on our skates. (Alison had taken me to the mall earlier to buy brand-new ones when I told her our plans!) Paige had agreed to meet Tyler there around seven. She'd invited Britnee and me to come along.

(Sarika wasn't with us anymore, because her father had gotten transferred to Scranton and they'd moved over winter vacation. I had kind of moved into her place.)

"Oh, great," Paige said sarcastically, taking off her short boots as she stared across the pond. "Look who's stalking us again."

Cat was sitting on a park bench, all by herself, almost directly across from us. She was wearing a baseball cap, army-type lace-up boots, and a long, black, wool coat, which looked weird since everyone else was dressed for skating.

Paige angrily pulled off her gloves. "Did you tell her we were coming, Ronnie?"

"What?" I couldn't believe she would ask me that. "Of course not!"

And I hadn't, because the more I fit in with them, the more obvious it became that Cat didn't. But that didn't prevent me from feeling guilty for not telling Cat where I was going when she'd shown up after dinner at my door.

"Want to go down to the ice pond, Ronnie?"

"No. I mean, maybe later . . . Paige said we might go to the movies. I'm not sure."

"Call me if you change your mind, okay?"

Poor Cat. As she stood up and began walking gingerly on the ice, she shielded her eyes from the bright lights as if searching for a familiar face. Luckily, a family with three kids sat down right in front of us, blocking us from her view. I lost sight of her as she started in the direction of the bridge and wondered if it would be just as easy to avoid her later.

My fingers were freezing as I tugged on my skates. I tried to hurry, blowing on my hands to keep them warm. Paige looked up and I noticed Jon skating toward us. He was holding a hockey stick under the arm of his puffy blue jacket.

"Hey, Jon!" called Paige. "Over here!"

Jon was Tyler's best friend. His hockey skates made a whooshing noise as he did a sharp stop right in front of us. "Tyler sent me to find you. He's already by the fire."

When he took off his knit cap, Jon's sweaty hair stuck to his forehead. He held out his hand as Paige tied her laces tight. She giggled as she grabbed for him, almost making him lose his balance.

"Meet me over there!" she called to us before she skated away, her matching pink scarf fluttering behind her.

Britnee and I took turns pulling each other as we skated along—it was so much fun. She knows how to skate backward, a rhythmic movement in the shape of a letter S. (I wish I knew how to skate like that.) As we darted through the crowd, I noticed in some places the ice had deep ruts in it from people skating hard or from twigs frozen in place. You had to be careful not to trip.

It was smoky when we got near the bonfire, and it smelled like burning leaves. Ashes and hot cinders flew up from the large can, glowing hot and red. There were about five or six kids standing around trying to get warm.

Tyler was behind Paige with his arms around her posses-
sively; they were definitely more than just friends. His
face was burrowed into her neck as she leaned back into
him, smiling.

"Come over here, Ronnie," Paige called, when she
saw me. "Hurry the hell up."

Sometimes I get tired of her ordering me around, but
I skated over anyway.

"Do you think she's drunk?" said Paige, nodding
toward the bridge.

"Who?"

I turned and there was Cat, standing in the middle of
the ice underneath the low steel bridge. Her long coat
was unbuttoned and open. A group of three boys—
including Jon—were taking turns skating past her. As
they did, they would knock her baseball hat off onto the
ice, and hit it around with their hockey sticks like it was
a puck.

"Cut it out!" she said laughing, her big breasts jig-
gling as she reached for her hat. "Give it back!" she
yelled.

"Watch what happens next," said Paige.

The crazy thing was that as Cat bent over to pick up
her hat, Jon came and grabbed her from behind! Once he
got a free feel, he quickly skated under the bridge. Then,
after a few minutes, another boy skated up to her and did
the same thing!

She screamed when they touched her—but she was
also laughing, so it didn't seem like she truly minded. She
was stumbling, too—slipping and falling—so it made me
wonder if Paige was right. Could Cat be drunk?

"Stop it!" she shouted, but not seriously. "Come on,
you guys, *please*!"

"Somebody needs a lot of attention," said Britnee, taking a lip gloss out of her pocket and gliding it over her mouth.

"Tyler thinks she's disgusting, right?" said Paige.

Tyler nodded and smiled, but I wasn't so sure. He'd been staring at Cat with those same slit eyes, like when he teased me about my bra size.

I shivered and moved closer to the fire.

Tyler was wearing a black ski jacket with a red spider stitched on the sleeve. He pulled a small bottle out of the side pocket and unscrewed the top. "Want some whiskey, Ronnie? It'll warm you right up."

Paige was giving me a look like I'd better say no because she thought that girls who drank with guys were sluts; but that was okay, I didn't want any alcohol.

"No thanks."

"How about you, pretty Pagers?" he said, offering the bottle to her.

She shook her head and said no. "But you can."

"Only if you'll skate with me." Tyler swallowed a big gulp then put the bottle back in his pocket. "Later," he said to us, grabbing Paige's hand suddenly. She shrieked as he pulled her away.

"Wait!" she yelled back to us. "Don't leave without me!"

I watched as they skated under the bridge until their shadowy figures disappeared around the corner. A few minutes later, the other boys left too, which meant, I guess, that their stupid game was finally over. As soon as they were gone, Cat trudged over to where we were standing.

"Can you believe those guys?" she asked. Close up she didn't seem drunk, just excited. "I told them to stop. They just wouldn't listen!"

Britnee was making a face, like, *you seriously expect us to believe that?* so I didn't say anything.

"Jon asked if I wanted to go sit with him—in his brother's car," Cat said, smiling, as she buttoned her coat. "Do you think I should?"

Could she really be that naive?

I rolled my eyes. "Do you think that's actually, like . . . *smart?*"

"Maybe you're right." She chewed her bottom lip, which was chapped, white, and flaky. "Maybe I should just go home. Want to come with me, Ronnie?"

Britnee shot me another look like, *why is she even talking to us?*

"No thanks," I said. "We promised to wait here for Paige."

Cat tried again. "Well, what about later?"

This was getting embarrassing. I gave her a look which meant, *shut up right now.* "No. I think I'm busy later."

"Why? Are you going to the *movies?*" she asked, with an accusing stare.

"No, but she's gonna be busy for the next hundred years," Britnee replied.

Cat tried to act like it didn't bother her, but I could see a shadow of disappointment cross her face. "Okay, I'll see you guys around, I guess."

She took a pair of headphones out of her coat pocket. As I watched her dark silhouette walk away, she looked lonely and big, and round and sad.

Just then Jennafer skated up right behind us. She was wearing a light blue ski cap, which had fake brown braids that hung next to her rosy cheeks. "I just heard about Cat and those boys!"

"Her family is *très* dysfunctional," said Britnee. "Didn't her brother go to jail?"

"Her mother's boyfriend," I said, wanting to show them I knew something they didn't. "He likes guns."

Jennafer shook her head. "What kind of a mother brings home a boyfriend who's been to jail?"

Britnee gave her a look like, *what do you expect?*

I felt bad all of a sudden, talking about Cat's family. "Sometimes people do things because they have no other choice. It doesn't necessarily make them bad people."

I thought about my mother and all the choices she'd had to make. What if Cat's mother was the same way, caught in her bad choices . . . sort of like a twig in the ice? Cat might be trapped like that, too.

"Why do you always stick up for her?" asked Jennafer.

I felt my face get hot. "No, I don't. Not really."

"Yes, you do," said Britnee, looking annoyed. "Like just now. Why did she ask you to come over? It was like you go over there all the time."

I shrugged. "Some people never give up, I guess."

Britnee stared at me suspiciously. "Are you still hanging out with her, Ronnie? Because if you are, I mean, don't you think we would have a problem with that?"

I didn't say anything, but I had a nervous feeling as I watched Cat walking up the snowy hill in the darkness, slipping away into the night.

January 23

Last night it snowed really hard. Ten inches: practically a blizzard. We didn't have school, but Alison went to work anyway, because even though a big snowstorm was nice for the kids, it didn't keep her patients from being depressed.

I crawled out of bed around lunchtime, made myself a tuna sandwich, and watched some TV. Then I bundled up in my new ski jacket (with the rabbit fur trim) and went outside to shovel the rest of the driveway and the walk.

I took Lucky with me because he loves to play in the snow. It was fun to throw a shovelful of fresh powder onto his back, and watch him run around like crazy shaking it off. I made a small snowman near the front stoop (for Alison) and stuck some twigs at his sides for arms. The noisy city plows with their flashing yellow lights went by three times in a row; Lucky surprised me by barking at them when they passed.

It was late afternoon when Cat came along wearing her long black coat and lace-up army boots. As soon as she got here, she threw herself down into the snow, and Lucky licked her all over her face. She let him chase after her, making crisscrossing paths in our front yard. With her arms flapping around in that long coat of hers, she reminded me of a big, black crow.

"Hey. Can you come over to my house?" she asked, completely out of breath. "There's something I want to show you."

I hadn't been to her house in almost a month. It seemed too creepy to be around Bud after what she'd told me, but she insisted he would leave us alone if I was there.

"Please? I promise it'll be fun."

I stuck the shovel in a big pile of snow by the garage and put Lucky inside, locking the door behind me.

The streetlights came on as we walked through the cold, deserted streets. We saw a few lopsided snowmen, plastic sleds set next to back doors, and neighbors getting dinner ready in their lighted kitchens. It was quiet, almost serene, until we got to Cat's house, that is.

We opened the door to the volume turned way up on the TV and the banging of drums from the basement. Cat said to keep my jacket on because her house was chilly, but we stomped our feet and put our boots on the mat just inside.

Cat's mother, Karen, was lying on the couch, wearing an orange and black shirt (her Home Depot work clothes). There was an infomercial on the TV, and littered around the couch were piles of newspapers and old *People* magazines.

"Oh, hello, girls," she said, using the remote to lower the volume. "How's the weather out there?"

The drumming in the basement stopped before we could answer, and we heard thudding footsteps coming up the stairs. Bud, wearing a plaid shirt with jeans, and a rubber band at his chin (around the hair of his short goatee), went past us without saying a word.

"Is it still bitter cold?" Karen asked, watching him go into the kitchen.

"It's cold," I replied, "but the streets are clear."

"Oh, good. Then I won't have much trouble getting to work."

"Karen!" Bud yelled from the kitchen. "There's

nothing to eat in this goddamn house! Get up and make me something, you lazy *pig*."

I got a nervous feeling, like maybe I should get out of there.

"What?" her mom called, as if pretending she didn't hear him might make us do the same. She sat up on the couch looking embarrassed.

I shot a glance at Cat who shrugged like this was nothing new.

"He's just crabby," her mom said anxiously. "His gig was canceled last night because of the storm."

"He always talks like that," Cat mumbled.

"No, he doesn't," said Karen. "Watch your mouth, Bud! Cathy's friend is here."

"You watch *your* mouth, *pig!*" he yelled back.

Karen got off the couch and hurried into the kitchen, where we could hear the opening and shutting of cabinets and the beeping sounds of a microwave. Finally, Bud stormed past us again, slamming the basement door as he went back downstairs; he was carrying a beer and some food on a paper plate. Cat's mom came out and leaned against the kitchen door.

"Nice," Cat said, shaking her head. "We're going up to my room."

"Have fun, girls," she replied, with a sad look in her eyes.

We walked past a heap of laundry in the hallway, three pairs of dirty sneakers, a curling iron, and the browning core of an apple on top of another magazine. I followed Cat up the stairs, which were also cluttered with newspapers, empty CD cases, and more shoes.

When we got to her room, Cat's mother called upstairs again. "I'm leaving now!" she yelled. "There's a frozen pizza in the freezer. Be good for Bud. See you!"

"Okay," Cat yelled back. "Bye."

We went into her room and Cat flicked on a small lamp on her desk. We took off our coats and tossed them onto her bed. I noticed she had something new on her wall, a black-and-white poster of staircases going in all different directions. Cat rolled her computer chair from her desk and put it in front of her door, under the door-knob, blocking it so nobody could get in. I gave her a look like, *is that because of him?*

She shook her head. "It's not what you think." She went behind her dresser and pulled out a paper bag with an old videotape inside it. She took the movie out of the box and put it into the VCR slot on the small television set on her dresser.

"We're going to watch a movie?"

"You'll see in a second," she explained. Holding the remote in her hand, she turned on the TV, which cast a blue light in the room. She fast-forwarded past the credits and a few of the beginning scenes. "Almost there. Just wait. Here."

At first it looked like a normal movie: some regular guy over at his girlfriend's house, and she was making him dinner. Steak. Mashed potatoes. Candles on the table. Then she brought him into the bedroom and there was *another* girl in the bed, totally naked. The guy had his clothes off so incredibly quickly after that . . . and then weird breathing and then . . .

OH MY GOD! THIS WAS A PORN MOVIE!

"What the hell, Cat! Turn it off!"

She hit the Pause button. It paused on a shot of the man's foot and the woman's face in the background.

"I found it in my mom's bedroom closet. Can you

believe it? Her and Bud actually watch this stuff." Cat lay back on her pillow with the remote pointed at the television again. "I knew you'd be shocked. Ready for more?"

Outside her window, it was completely dark. I heard another snowplow with its beeping back-up sound on the street below. I pictured our house just blocks away, with Alison coming home from work soon, and Lucky waiting to be fed.

"No, it's gross."

Cat smiled nervously. "But you've just got to see this next part. It's hilarious."

Hilarious?

I didn't *think* so. What was with her, anyway? She was turning into someone I seriously didn't know at all.

"No thanks. I have to go." I grabbed my jacket and began pushing my arms through the sleeves. "I just remembered something I have to do."

"Wait. Don't leave yet." Her face crumpled. "Don't be like that."

I zipped my jacket and threw my scarf around my neck. "Like what?"

"Acting like you're better than me. Your family is screwed up too. You and me, we're exactly the same."

"Whatever." Even if that was true, there was no way I was going to sit there and watch that stupid movie with her. I moved the chair and hurried downstairs, praying that I wouldn't run into Bud as I pulled on my boots and flew out the door.

When I got back to the house, all the lights were on downstairs. I found Alison sitting in the living room;

she was wearing her slippers and reading the newspaper. On her lap was a white knitted blanket, and she'd started a fire in the fireplace. Lucky was curled up on the Oriental rug next to her rocking chair. His tail thumped when he saw me come in, but he didn't get up; he must have been tired from all the fresh air.

I walked over and petted his head. "Hey, boy."

"Where have you been?" asked Alison, putting down the paper. "I was starting to worry. You didn't leave me a note."

"I didn't think you'd be home yet. I went over to Cat's."

"Oh." She seemed relieved. "One of my patients canceled on me. Thanks for shoveling, I really appreciate it. What were you girls up to?"

"Nothing." I sat down next to the fireplace and tried to warm up my feet. "It was boring. I left after her mom went to work."

Alison seemed surprised. "Good decision! I thought we'd have some spaghetti tonight, okay?"

I smiled. "No, please, not again!"

Alison laughed. She knew I was joking. She made the best spaghetti *ever*. I'd even begun calling the sauce she poured over it "gravy" like she did—a Pennsylvania Dutch expression. She got up from the couch and began walking toward the kitchen.

I relaxed into a throw pillow, feeling the warmth of the fireplace, and closed my eyes. It felt so good to be home.

Home?

Funny, it *did* feel like my home all of a sudden. So different from Cat's house; it was always chaotic there, crazy. Why had I told Alison it was boring at

Cat's? If anything it was boring *here*, with just me and Alison and Lucky, and the fire and Alison's great cooking and peace and quiet and . . .

I suddenly realized that I liked that feeling: *boring*. I wanted it to last. And just like that I made my decision.

"Hey, Alison?" I called, hoping she'd come back into the room.

She poked her head out of the kitchen. "What is it, dear?"

"I want you to go ahead and file."

"What?" She looked so startled that she almost dropped the box of spaghetti on the floor. "Are you saying what I think you're—?"

I nodded. "I like it here. I want to stay."

January 26

My mother didn't show up today at her social worker's office for our regular monthly phone call. Midge claimed that Mom was sick with the flu, but I knew for a fact that sometimes my mother would get very sick after a weeklong binge, so I didn't really believe it.

Midge glanced at her calendar, trying to set up another appointment. As I looked out the window, watching the winter rain wash away all the snow, I felt relieved. It wasn't right that my mother had ditched me, but a part of me was glad. The whole day I had been worried with this nervousness in the pit of my stomach about how I was going to tell my mother (or *not* tell her) that I'd decided to let Alison try to adopt me. I'd been a wreck about what her reaction might be.

But then I got to thinking, maybe she'd already

found out. Maybe Midge had told her. Maybe that was the real reason she wasn't there for our call. Maybe she'd given up on me. Maybe she didn't have any other choice.

February 13

Lucky got loose!

I was hysterical. I could hardly breathe! The first thing I did was call Alison, who was in the middle of a session with a patient. She told me to stop hyperventilating and tell her what was wrong. After I did, she got panicky herself and promised to hurry home right after she was through.

We have this chain staked into the ground outside our side door, where we put Lucky when it's too cold to take him for a walk—or if we just don't feel like going outside. That's where I accidentally left him this morning. When I got home from school today and he wasn't in the house like he was supposed to be, I suddenly remembered what I must have done. And then I almost threw up.

How did it happen?

Alison left early this morning because she had to be in court to file a motion to get custody of me, which is the first legal step toward adoption. While I ate breakfast, I tried to get Paige on the phone because she hadn't called me back last night, and she was sort of distant to me in school yesterday. I had a funny feeling that somebody (somebody named *Britnee*) had told Paige that Cat and I were still friends.

Were they planning to ignore me again?

I didn't think I could take it.

I decided that this sneaking-around-being-Cat's-friend business HAD TO STOP. It was just too risky. This was the final straw. No matter how sorry I felt for her I couldn't take the chance. No more phone calls. No more going over to her crazy house. No more Cat!

But how would I ever get her to agree?

As I finished my cereal, I tried Paige again. Her mother told me to stop calling already and couldn't it wait until I saw her at school? I tried to tell Mrs. Jamison that it was crucially important—I only needed to talk to Paige for one teeny tiny little second without everyone around. Her mother said, "Well, fine, she'll call you back."

Paige never did call, but when I saw her later at the bus stop, she treated me just fine. She said that she's had cramps with her period for over two weeks straight, so that explains why she's been in such a bad mood, I guess.

Of course with all that going on this morning, *anybody* would've had to rush around like crazy in order to make the bus and *anybody* might have forgotten to bring Lucky back inside.

It was freezing outside today with drizzling, icy rain. Lucky, I'm sure, got tired of waiting for me. Somehow he'd managed to chew through his rope, because there it was lying on the ground next to the door. He was probably as cold as an ice cube and soaking wet besides. I'm sure he was feeling scared to death and lonely and forgotten.

Please, please, please, God, I prayed after I found out he was missing, please help me find him.

As soon as I got off the phone with Alison, I ran around the block once or twice calling out his name. I

even stopped at Cat's house because I thought somebody there might have seen him. I was desperate. But
nobody was home. So when I got back I called and left
her a message, just in case. "If you get this, Cat, call
me," I sobbed. "Lucky ran away!"

Next, I called Francis. God must have heard my
prayers because Francis was actually in his office and
not out teaching a class (he teaches Philosophy of
Religion at Alvernia College). He said to make a list of
all the places that Lucky might have gone, places that
were familiar, and he would be right over to help look
for him.

In the meantime I couldn't stop thinking about how
much I loved Lucky and also (this was the worst part) if
maybe Lucky was dead. Why I was thinking such dark
thoughts, I don't know. I guess it's what people do when
tragedy strikes; they automatically prepare themselves
for the worst. I actually pictured where we would bury
him (under the tire swing in the side yard) and what his
gravestone would say:

HERE LIES LUCKY.
DIED TOO SOON.
ALL RONNIE'S FAULT.

But maybe . . . it wasn't . . . *completely* my fault.

Francis arrived in five seconds (not really, but he
was pretty fast). I told him how Lucky being gone was
really . . . probably . . . mostly . . . all because of *Cat*.

"If I hadn't been so stressed out wondering how I
was going to get her out of my life," I explained, "then
none of this would have happened."

Francis got very quiet. "You didn't leave Lucky outside on purpose, but that doesn't change a thing. *You*
were the one who let Lucky down, Ronnie. And for

what it's worth, it sounds like you're letting your friend down, too."

"Thanks," I said, making a face. "Like I don't feel bad enough."

He frowned. "Well, you're certainly not acting like it."

We got into his car and circled the neighborhood, and then we drove to the park near the high school. Dark wet leaves were pressed up against the wire fence at the ball field like puppies' noses in a pet store window. Lucky wasn't anywhere to be found, so we began to drive back home.

I felt pretty hopeless at this point. We were running out of ideas.

"Maybe you could make some flyers, Ronnie? And post them around the neighborhood?"

"What about putting something in the newspaper, too?"

"It couldn't hurt," Francis replied.

Just as we turned the corner, we saw Alison driving down our street. She opened her window a crack and said she'd join us, but that she would leave her car at home.

As soon as we pulled up to the house, Cat showed up looking worried.

"Oh my God, poor Lucky!" she cried. "I'm not going home till we find him."

I guessed we could use all the help we could get, but as it turned out we didn't need her help.

As soon as Alison opened the garage door to park her car, Lucky came running out all excited and wagging his happy tail. He'd been in the garage the whole time!

I couldn't get out of the car fast enough. We bent down and Lucky licked each one of us on our face. Then he jumped up like he always does to hug us around our legs. I held onto him so tightly that Alison said, "Be careful, Ronnie. You're hurting him." But she seemed just thrilled and even gave Francis a big hug. When she did that, Francis winked at me and I got all happy inside.

But Cat was being totally annoying as usual. She kept calling, "Here, boy!" every time Lucky came over to me—acting like he was *her* dog or something. I was wishing she'd go home, so no one would see her standing outside my house.

After a few minutes, I tried making a strong suggestion. "Didn't you say you had to go home and fix dinner or something?"

Cat shrugged. "No hurry. Just frozen pizza—and nobody to eat it with—*again*."

(Talk about fishing for an invitation.)

"That doesn't sound very appetizing," said Francis, stamping his feet in the cold.

"Would you care to join us, dear?" said Alison, grabbing a grocery bag from the front seat of her car.

(They were such pushovers.)

"Maybe you could go home and get your movies?" I said sarcastically, but nobody knew what I was talking about—except Cat, who secretly smiled at me as if she'd won again.

We planned to eat in the dining room since Alison said that finding Lucky was a special occasion. I set the table with the good dishes as she sliced the pot roast and Francis prepared a salad.

After we sat down, Alison filled our glasses with sparkling cider, and Francis made a toast. "To Lucky's safe return!"

"Yippee!" said Cat loudly, raising her glass.

I gave her a dirty look.

"I have another announcement to make," said Alison, passing the basket of bread. "This morning the judge granted me permanent custody of you, Ronnie. Your adoption hearing is set for June!"

"That's wonderful news," said Francis, reaching for her hand. "Congratulations."

He turned to smile at me. "You must be so excited."

That's when the strangest thing happened. Suddenly I couldn't look either of them in the eye. You'd think I'd be grateful for the chance to live a wonderful life with Alison, but I wasn't. It was almost like as soon as I saw the door slamming shut on my mother, a part of me wanted to kick it back open again.

Before I could say anything, Cat, of course, had to interfere. "But her mom could still try for her, right?"

Francis and Alison shot each other a look.

Cat stared at me. "Didn't you tell them how much you want to live up there?" she continued. "How much you miss your little brothers?"

"Jeez, Cat," I said. "Please shut up!"

The only sound you could hear was the clinking of forks on our plates.

Nobody said a word.

This was a perfect example of why I don't want to be friends with her anymore. We'd had that conversation over a month ago, when yes, I was feeling that way.

Alison stopped eating and put a napkin to her lips. "I spent over two and a half hours in court today, Ronnie. Now is the time to speak up, if you're not really sure."

"No," I answered. "I want you to adopt me, honest. This is just hard for me. A big adjustment. A whole new way of thinking."

Francis nodded. "Does it feel like you're being disloyal to your old family?"

"Sometimes."

"Completely understandable," he replied.

Alison sighed like she sometimes did when Francis would know the perfect thing to say. I tried to smile, but now there was a huge damper on our celebration—all because of Cat.

Then Cat, the big mouth, tried changing the subject. "So how do you think Lucky got into the garage?"

We found out right after dinner.

While Cat and I were clearing the table, our next-door neighbor (Mr. Peterman, who owns Peterman's Tires) called to say that he had seen Lucky off his leash, running around our yard in the icy rain. Mr. Peterman used the spare key that Alison had given him (in case we were ever locked out) to put Lucky in our garage "out of the weather." He hoped we didn't mind, and didn't think to call us any sooner; he'd just assumed I'd hear Lucky barking when I got home.

I guess Mr. Peterman didn't know that Lucky seldom barks—border collies hardly ever do—and as for looking for him in the garage? Well, why the heck would I? But thank goodness for Mr. Peterman anyway, because now the mystery was solved, and Lucky wasn't dead, and I was on my way to having a real home at last. I was thinking that I probably wouldn't ask God for a single solitary thing for the next twenty years.

Except maybe for some help with getting Cat out of my life.

(For good this time.)

February 28

Paige finally invited me for a sleepover last night!

Alison was nice enough to let me go, even though Paige's parents wouldn't be home, so what could be more perfect? Of course, Alison first insisted on questioning Mrs. Jamison on what the arrangements would be, and only after I'd promised to check in with her like every hour by cell phone did she say it was okay.

"Don't make me regret this decision," Alison said. "I'm trusting you."

I smiled. "I promise I won't let you down."

Dr. and Mrs. Jamison left around six that evening for a medical convention in New York City. Paige's sister, Marissa, was coming home later that night from college—but not till eleven. (She was driving all the way up from Virginia and the traffic was supposedly bad on Friday nights.) Her mom and dad said Paige could pick two friends to keep her company, and since she was so responsible, they weren't worried at all.

When Britnee and I arrived, the Jamisons pulled out of the driveway, waving good-bye from their black Mercedes-Benz. Paige greeted us at the door. We put our shoes into the wicker basket they kept near the closet for just that purpose.

Paige's house was beautiful and glamorous inside, almost like one of those houses that a movie star might live in. Everything was white, even the furniture and the carpeting and their dog (a toy poodle named Trixie). I'm sure there were other colors in her house too, but white was the prevalent theme.

(Or at least it was, until after the party—but I'll get to that!)

We went up the white-carpeted circular staircase and put our sleepover stuff in her room. Paige's bedroom had a TV, a computer, a DVD player, and a refrigerator built right into her bookshelves—in case she got thirsty in the middle of the night! She slept in a brass bed under a lace canopy with a purple-flowered comforter and sheets that were made of "one-hundred percent Egyptian cotton," because, Paige told us, her skin was so very sensitive.

While Britnee and Paige sat underneath that beautiful lace canopy trying to decide what to do, I sat on one of the fluffy pillows on the floor. None of us could come up with anything that didn't sound completely boring until Paige said, "I think we should have a party."

"Oooooh," said Britnee, clapping her hands. "What a great idea."

"Awesome," I said, but in the back of my mind I was thinking, is she crazy?

"It's been too long since I've had a party," said Paige, sighing. "I deserve to have some fun."

As she yawned, her flat stomach peeked out from between her pink sweater and her jeans. "But won't you get in trouble if your parents find out?" I asked.

(I wasn't crazy about the possibility of Alison finding out either.)

"Only a few chosen people will be invited," Paige said smugly as she picked up the phone. "Just Tyler and some of his friends. Don't be such a worry-queen, Ronnie. We won't get caught."

The party went remarkably well—at first. Tyler brought Jon and Marshall with him, two friends from the basketball team. (Jon was the kid from skating a few weeks ago and Marshall was very tall and thin, with freckles and brown eyes and a buzz cut.) The boys sat around drinking from a six-pack of Coors Light, which Tyler had carried in from the Jamisons' garage. This made me nervous, but Paige said they promised not to drink too much. Britnee and I went into the kitchen and baked brownies while Paige set out the chips.

Once the brownies were done, we watched the guys play pool in the den, until somebody turned down the lights. Tyler and Paige began making out on the brown leather couch in the corner while the rest of us tried not to notice.

I almost kissed Marshall, but then decided he wasn't all that cute—his nose was wide and bumpy like a pickle, and he had acne besides. Jon and Britnee sat next to each other on the love seat, holding hands. After about fifteen uncomfortable minutes of watching Paige and Tyler making out, I guess we'd all had enough.

"Hey. Why don't you guys get a room?" said Jon, laughing.

"He's right," said Tyler, putting his arm around Paige. "I've never been upstairs."

I thought Paige looked nervous, but she said okay. Britnee and I exchanged glances as he led her away.

As soon as they left, Jon got up from the couch and popped open another can of beer. "This party is lame. We need more people. I'm calling my brother."

"Party!" shouted Marshall.

Were they serious? Without even asking Paige?

"I'm not sure that's such a great idea," I said.

"Okay, *Mom*," said Jon sarcastically. "Everybody raise your hand if you care."

Britnee looked at me like she *did* care, but she couldn't say anything because she sort of liked Jon.

Obviously nobody raised their hands, so Jon got out his cell phone and began calling people—just like that. They even made a joke about inviting Cat. (Maybe they thought they could use her somehow—but thankfully they didn't have her number.)

After only ten minutes, kids started showing up at the door, older kids, because Jon's brother was in high school and he could drive.

In no time at all the party got louder and louder, and more crowded, and after about an hour it was pretty much out of control. No one was putting their shoes into the wicker basket by the front door, so they all dragged in mud from outside. There were beer cans on every available table, and some just strewn on the floor.

I couldn't believe it! It was so upsetting and I didn't know what to do. There was spilled popcorn and chips and the brownies we'd made (what was left of them) were getting crushed into the white carpet. Kids were jumping off the pool table and throwing darts at the pictures on the wall. It was pure chaos.

Just when I thought it couldn't get any worse, the first kid started throwing up.

It was Britnee. She was totally drunk!

"Sorry," she said, holding her hair out of the way. "I think I'm gonna be sick!"

Right after she puked, some other kids started puking too!

The smell of it made me gag and I felt my stomach clench. I went to the kitchen to get a wet sponge and some paper towels, but then I thought, why should I have to clean up *that*? Where was Paige? This was *her* house that was getting trashed.

Just then my cell phone began to vibrate in my

pocket. I looked at the number . . . Alison! I had to go outside where it wasn't noisy and try to make my voice sound neutral and calm.

"Hello?"

"Do you girls need anything?" she asked. "A movie? Some pizza?"

"No, nothing, we're fine. Thanks for asking, though."

When I got off the phone I realized she might just drive by and check up on us. I had better do something, *fast*.

I went back inside and ran up those circular stairs and pounded on Paige's bedroom door, which was shut tight. But it was so noisy with the music blaring from downstairs that I guess she couldn't hear me. When she didn't answer, I took a deep breath, hoped this wouldn't be too embarrassing for any of us, and pushed open the door.

Paige and Tyler were lying on her bed on top of her purple-flowered comforter. Tyler had his shirt off, and Paige was underneath him. Her sweater was halfway up her back, but at least she was still wearing it, along with her jeans.

Tyler noticed me first. His sweaty face was twisted like, *get lost, Ronnie*.

"I'm really sorry to interrupt, but—"

"What's the matter?" said Paige, peering over his shoulder. "This had *better* be good."

"There are about a hundred kids downstairs," I said anxiously. "And some of them are throwing up."

"Oh my God!" She quickly sat up and pulled down her sweater.

"Does this mean we have to stop?" asked Tyler, leaning back on a pillow.

Paige gave him a look like, *what is* wrong *with you?*

We ran downstairs and Paige tried to break up the party, but most of the kids ignored her, even though at this point Paige was running through the crowd screaming, "Get out of my house! Get the *hell* out of my house!"

After about five minutes of no luck whatsoever in trying to end this stupid party (because half of the people there were too drunk to care), take one guess who came walking through the front door?

Paige's sister, Marissa, and her boyfriend, Ryan, that's who. They were carrying two leather duffel bags and their backpacks from college. I glanced at my watch. It wasn't even nine thirty!

Marissa was an older version of Paige, with the same dark hair, only shorter, and those same turquoise eyes, and an incredibly beautiful face. Except at the moment, it was a very angry face.

"What the *hell!*" Marissa shouted. "I just *knew* we'd better get here early. Look at this place! This is our *house*, Paige. You are in *so* much trouble."

Paige was hyperventilating. "Please! I don't even know half these people! You've got to believe me. I didn't invite them. They just showed up!"

(But obviously, we both knew that if she hadn't insisted on having this party in the first place, there was no way she'd be in this mess.)

Paige stared at me with those big you've-got-to-help-me-out-here eyes.

"She's right, Marissa," I said, trying to sound convincing. "We've been trying to get rid of them for like an hour!"

Marissa turned off the music, and Ryan told the kids to leave right now or he would call the police—or their parents. Everybody cleared out so fast you wouldn't believe it, but the place was still a wreck.

Marissa made sure none of the drivers were drunk, and after they shoved the last kid out the door, Marissa and her boyfriend picked up their duffel bags and began to walk up the stairs, leaving the three of us (Paige, Britnee, and me) behind with all the mess.

The house looked awful. Like the aftermath of a terrible disaster; maybe a hurricane or a flood.

Paige rubbed her eyes and shook her head in disbelief. "Wait, Marissa. Aren't you even going to *help*?"

"Not my problem," her sister replied, giving us an icy stare. "It was a long drive. We're going upstairs to relax."

"But Marissa!"

They continued to ignore her, and Paige began to whine. "But you don't understand. I don't know how to *clean!*"

"Look," Marissa said. "If you work hard at it, Mom and Dad will never be able to tell. And if you keep your big mouth shut about Ryan sleeping in my room tonight, they probably won't hear it from me."

Paige was right; she didn't even know how to turn on the vacuum cleaner. After Marissa went upstairs, Britnee put her hand over her mouth, clutched her stomach, and abruptly ran into the bathroom again, where she stayed for the next hour. So who do you think had to vacuum up popcorn and scrub brownie stains out of the rug in the den while Paige lounged on the couch offering lame advice?

I was ready to slug her as she pointed out stray beer cans on the windowsills, or spots of throw up on the floor. It was disgusting, and I wondered, why the hell am I doing this?

But somehow Paige made up for it by being hysterically funny. She made fun of some of the people at the party, her sister, and even did a great imitation of Miss Riley at school. Britnee came out of the bathroom to find the two of us laughing so hard that tears were streaming down our faces.

After we brought the garbage outside, we went upstairs and collapsed on Paige's canopy-covered bed and she told us all about how she had put her tongue right into Tyler's mouth and how it felt soooo good. We screamed extremely loud when she said that!

Marissa yelled from her bedroom down the hall, "*Shut up!*"

"Tyler tried to feel me up, too," Paige whispered, "but I only let him on the outside, because I don't want to be a slut."

The next morning Marissa was up early and she made us pancakes for breakfast, which was really sweet, considering she had been pretty mean the night before. She told us we did an awesome job of cleaning (except for a few spots on the rug) and said that she was fairly sure their parents wouldn't notice. And she even offered to tell them she'd had a few friends over if any of the neighbors mentioned seeing a crowd. Wasn't that the nicest?

Before I knew it Alison was honking the horn in the driveway. I found my shoes in the basket and grabbed my sleepover stuff. I called good-bye to Paige, who was talking to Tyler on her cell. I thought she might be too busy to say good-bye, but she was suddenly standing very close behind me. "Thanks, Ronnie," she whispered. "For *everything*. I'll call you later. You're the *best*."

Then she hugged me so tightly that I thought, what does she mean?

Could we possibly be turning into *best* friends?

March 17

HAPPY ST. PATRICK'S DAY!!!

Tonight Alison and Francis and I went out to dinner at an Irish pub. Everything they served at O'Malley's was green in honor of St. Pat's—like green mashed potatoes and green Jell-O—almost everything but the meat, which was corned beef (*disgusting*), so I had a salad instead, which was, naturally, green.

A folk singer was playing an acoustic guitar. Did I mention that Francis is half Irish? He and Alison each had a glass of green beer—but only one. Francis was talking about how excited he was that spring was coming and how he couldn't wait to start gardening again. Alison replied that she dreaded the thought of having to mow the lawn and that digging in the dirt wasn't her idea of fun.

During dinner they started asking questions, trying to pry out of me what I remembered about my past. They've been doing that **A LOT** lately. I guess they want to get more information just in case my mother tries to contest this adoption, because, according to Midge, she still hasn't signed the papers "terminating her parental rights."

Mom missed last month's phone call *again*, which leads me to believe that she isn't going to try to stop us, so I don't know what they're so worried about. Still, why wouldn't my mother sign the stupid papers if she wasn't even going to bother talking to me?

I told Alison and Francis that when I lived with my mom, what I remember most is taking care of my brothers: Derek first, then Dan when he came along. I had to give Dan his bottle and I learned how to make macaroni and cheese.

Alison, of course, pumped me for more.

"Did your mom's boyfriend ever abuse you?" she asked. "Kenny, I mean?"

She'd only asked me this about a zillion times. "No," I said.

"Well, did he ever hurt your mother?" asked Francis.

"Are you counting the time he kicked her across the kitchen floor?"

Alison sadly shook her head because she already knew this from my file.

I don't like going back to my past. I try to block it out, but sometimes I do get a glimpse of other bad things that happened when I was living with them. Like a gypsy moth flapping around inside my brain, those memories are brown and dusty and hard to hold on to— and even if you could, would you really want to?

The truth is that I never got along with Kenny. It makes me cringe to think of the tattoo of a shark on his arm, and his long, greasy hair. One time I overheard him saying that he thought I was spoiled and strange. He blamed Raylene for brainwashing me, taking me to church, and teaching me all that "religious mumbo jumbo."

Mom made excuses for him—constantly. "He loves you, Ronnie. I swear. He's just under a lot of stress." (I guess it was stressful being a drug dealer.)

Kenny's brother lived in Alaska, and had promised

Kenny half his charter fishing business if we'd move up there. One night when they were packing boxes, I was showing Derek (who was five) how to play a new video game that Mom had bought to keep us occupied. Little Danny, who was running a fever, had just puked SpaghettiOs all over the fire truck in his playpen.

"Clean that mess up, Ronnie," Kenny shouted. "It smells."

"Why can't you do it?" I said, my thumb on the controller. "He's your kid."

Derek shot me a look like, *oh no, Sis. He's gonna be mad.*

"Because we're in the middle of packing!" Kenny yelled, exploding. He threw the masking tape against the wall. "*Christ.* Do it *now!*"

"You can't tell me what to do," I said, jumping out of the way. "You're not my real father." (I was older now, and had begun talking back to him to see if my mother would ever take my side.)

Mom ran out of the kitchen, holding a can of beer. She looked nervous. "Kenny, what's the problem? It's no big deal. I'll do it, okay?"

"No. Let me handle this," he replied, his eyes a cold, lifeless blue. "She's right. I'm not her real father. *Her* goddamn daddy's in jail."

He walked over to pick up the tape and then he came back and grabbed my chin. "So, little girl, that means you *have* to listen to me."

"No!" I said forcefully, pulling away. "I *never* will. You're going to hell, that's what Raylene says. And besides, my real father isn't in jail. My father is *God*, up in heaven!"

I'll never know where I got the nerve to say that. Maybe I wanted Kenny to hit me, so my mother would see how horrible he was, so she would make him go to Alaska all by himself.

He raised his thick arm like he was going to swing, but my mother quickly scooped Danny out of his playpen and jumped in between us. "No! Don't, Kenny. I swear!"

He glared at us, took his beer can off the table, and stormed out of the house.

Much later, when he finally came home, my mother and Kenny had an extremely huge fight. As I lay with my head under my covers (and my stuffed animals surrounding me) I could hear him shouting and throwing things in the next room. I peeked out long enough to pray to the statue of Scary Jesus on my dresser. Please, God, please, please make them stop. Then there was a weird quiet and a thud on the floor—and finally, my mother's muffled sobs.

I've always wondered if that's when she decided to leave without me.

March 19

After almost three months of not hearing a single word from her, I actually talked to my mother on the phone this afternoon in Midge's office! The first thing she did was apologize about not calling. "I've been in a halfway house. Since the end of January. They wouldn't let us make any long-distance calls."

Then she asked about a letter she had sent me about coming to live with her in Alaska. She's ready for **me** to come live with **her**? I can't believe it!

How did that happen? Why didn't anyone tell me?

"It's all in the letter," she said. "Didn't you even bother to read it?"

She claimed she had sent it right before she left for the halfway house and wondered why I hadn't written her back. She didn't want to pressure me, but now she sort of needed an answer if she was going to get a lawyer and all.

I was in a state of shock.

"I don't know what you're talking about, Mom."

"Fine, pretend all you want. I know she's filing for adoption. So I guess you've decided to stay with that Alison woman instead."

"Yes. But, I didn't realize you were—"

"Please," she replied. "Don't mess with my head."

"Look, I didn't get any *damn* letter, so that's why I didn't write you back."

She told me to *watch my mouth* and then said I should ask my caseworker about the letter. And she didn't want to talk anymore because it was making her too upset. "I'm not going to jeopardize my sobriety over this, Veronica. Let me know if you change your mind. But don't wait too long. I've got my own life to worry about."

When I hung up the phone and asked Midge about the letter, her penciled eyebrows started twitching and she said I should probably ask Alison. Then I asked Midge why she didn't tell me that my mom was in a halfway house and was trying to get me back, and she said she'd only found out two weeks ago herself.

Then why didn't she let me know two weeks ago?

There must be a full moon this week because it feels like all sorts of weird things are happening. First of all, there's my mother's letter, which I can't ask Alison about until she gets home from work—in about ten minutes, I think. And also, something very, very strange is going on with Cat.

Are you ready for this?

A few kids at school this morning mentioned that they heard she gave one of Tyler's friends a blow job!!!!!!

I happen to think that's a total and complete lie, because even though Cat is someone who craves attention, I can't believe she would stoop that low.

Where would they even do it?

It seems way too sketchy.

But then I remembered her bringing me over to her house to watch that porn movie. And the energy field around her has been different lately. Like just yesterday, I noticed Tyler and a bunch of his friends were kind of pushing into her in the hallway and trying to block her way. It was kind of like the night at the pond.

It was bothering me all day, so I asked her about the rumor in study hall.

"Are you serious?" Cat said, chewing on the tip of a pencil. "That's disgusting."

I wanted to believe her, but there was a moment of hesitation that ran across her face so that now I'm not totally sure. Then she asked if we could hang out this weekend. "Ronnie, we never spend time together anymore."

And so I promised to call her, but I was thinking, probably *not*.

Paige has been acting stressed out lately, too, because Tyler keeps pressuring her to do more and she's not sure she wants to because he's always flirting with other girls. It drives her crazy, but she also kind of wants to at the same time. They are fighting about it *constantly*, and all she wants to do is talk about it with us girls.

Boring and gross.

Who wants to hear the details (or *non*-details) of their stupid sex life?

Oops, there's the garage door opening. It's Alison. She just got home. GTG. Got To Go. BFN. Bye For Now.

Alison threw off her coat and rushed around the kitchen getting dinner ready, putting the black wok on the stove because we were going to have chicken stir-fry, which she knows is one of my favorite dinners *ever*. The yummy smell of frying peppers and onions quickly filled the room.

"I talked to my mother today!" I said excitedly.

"You did? It's been such a long time. Could you set the table, dear?"

She began slicing up the chicken at the cutting board.

I pulled open the silverware drawer. "I know. I know. *Finally*. But anyway, she was asking about a letter she sent me."

"A letter?"

Alison kept right on cutting up the chicken like it was no big deal; like I was telling her Lucky had the hiccups or asking her about lunch money for school.

"Yeah. She said she sent it awhile ago. Midge told me to ask you."

When Alison turned around, her face was pale, and

her hand, holding the kitchen knife, was shaking. "Ronnie, don't be too upset, okay?"

She went into the other room and brought back her briefcase and slowly began searching through it. Then she pulled one of those manila mailing envelopes from a zippered compartment and handed it to me.

"I didn't mean to keep it for so long," she said. "Sorry."

I took out the letter—**my mother's letter**—which I noticed right away had already been opened, so I knew Alison had read it—or at least she knew what it said.

I was completely shocked.

"It's been opened," I said, trying to stay calm.

Alison could barely meet my eyes. "Well, Midge always opens them, right?"

Suddenly it dawned on me that Alison must have kept it from me. On *purpose*!

"You read my mail, didn't you?"

"Well, it depends on how you look at—"

"You read my private mail. From my *mother*."

"I'm so sorry. What more can I say?" She looked the guiltiest I'd ever seen her.

I studied the postmark. "Not only did you read it, but you *kept* it from me. Look at this! She sent it like *weeks* ago!"

"Please, Ronnie. Midge said it got lost in the agency. I've only had it a short time myself. I didn't get it until the end of February."

(It was now the middle of March.)

"So when were you planning to give it to me? Next week? Next year? *Never*?"

Alison began talking really fast. "I didn't know if you were ready to handle it. I thought it might confuse things.

I wanted us to process it . . . *together*. How about this? Let's talk about it after dinner, after you calm down."

"Calm down? Calm down? You want *me* to calm down?" I was shouting right in her face.

"Please, stop." Alison backed away and lowered the flame on the stove. "Just take some time to read it. Then we can discuss it. After dinner, okay?"

I threw the letter onto the floor. "I don't have to read it, do I? I mean you've already read it for me, right? Why don't you just tell me what it says and then you can tell me what to do. You're obviously thinking for me now, too. Right?"

Her eyes filled with tears. "Please, put this in perspective. I love you, sweetheart. Very much. I only want what's best for you."

"What's *best* for me?"

That's when I seriously lost it.

"People who *love* each other don't keep secrets! They don't read each other's *private mail*! They don't try to manipulate a situation by trying to get it to come out the way *they* want it to. You don't love me, Alison. You say you do, but you don't! You just want to *friggin'* control me!"

With that, I bent over, picked up the letter, and stormed upstairs—leaving her to think about the terrible thing she had done to me.

Five minutes later

**I CAN'T BELIEVE WHAT JUST HAPPENED!!!!!!
I AM SO MAD I AM SHAKING!!!!!**

Here is the letter my mother sent me.

January 25
  Dear Ronnie,
    *My caseworker said I should write you about where
I'm going for the next couple of months, in case you don't
hear from me. I'll be in this halfway house so I can just
focus on myself and getting sober. Your brothers are with
one of my friends. I've been doing a lot of thinking and
you're right to be angry about what I put you through so
I've decided I'm going to try to get you back. It's either
now or I guess I'll lose you forever.*
    *My landlord said he will try to reserve one of them
bigger apartments for me if you want to come up here
and live with us. And Uncle Melvin said he might loan
me some money to get us started. That would still mean
you helping with chores and watching your brothers
when I go to work or to my AA meetings. I have to start
going to those meetings anyway when I get out or they
won't let me keep the boys.*
    *I wanted to send you this new picture. Derek is start-
ing to look like you, don't you think? At least how I
remember you looking when you were his age.*
    *My caseworker told me to be prepared, that you
might not want to come all the way up here to this cold
and lonely place. Do you want to be adopted by that
Alison woman instead?*
    *'Cause if you do, it would kill me inside, but I'd try to
understand and then I would sign those papers and stop
trying to fight for you.*
    *No matter what you decide I will still love you
because I'm your mother even though I haven't acted
much like one for all these years. Sorry!!!!!*
    Please write back and tell the truth—no matter what!
Love,
Mom

P.S. Danny colored this picture for you. It's supposed to be a bald eagle in a tree.

Alison knocked on my bedroom door several times, but now she's back downstairs. After I finished reading my mother's letter I started to cry, especially when I looked at the photograph of her sitting on that ratty old couch with my brothers so big I'm not sure I would recognize them if I passed them on the street.

But what really got to me was when I unfolded the drawing from little Danny. On the back, there was a red heart with the words, *We love you, Sis. Come home soon.*

It made me feel so lonely. My heart was *breaking*. My family seemed so far away because they *were* far away. Three *thousand* miles away. But somehow they had managed to find me and were loving me right here in my room.

Didn't Alison realize how much this was hurting me? How could she keep this letter from me? This letter changed *everything*! She must have known that it would. She didn't love me, not really. She was only thinking of herself. She was no different from anyone else who had betrayed me.

A few minutes later, I fell onto the bed and started pulling my hair. I pounded my fist against the headboard and inside my head I screamed, *No! No! No! No!*

A powerful rage came over me and before I knew it, I was throwing things around my room. Everything! All of the things that Alison had given me.

I cleared my dresser with one swoop of my hand.

I ripped the denim curtains off the windows.

I took all of my clothes out of my closet and tossed them on the floor.

But that wasn't enough, and more than that, it wasn't working. I realized I needed to do something REALLY BIG this time.

Something permanent. Hurtful. Important.

Then I saw the computer Alison had given me, sitting on my desk. If I destroyed it, I knew there would be no turning back.

I picked it up. The tall tower case was heavy.

I was going to throw the whole thing out the window, desperate to hear the sound of breaking glass. It was in my arms, I was ready to hurl it, but it wouldn't budge.

(That's because the power cords were still plugged into the back of the machine.)

So I sat down and unplugged them one by one.

But as I was unplugging them, I had time to think.

I didn't need to destroy my computer, I realized. There was something else I could do, instead. But I needed to do it quickly, before I changed my mind.

I got up from the chair and ran downstairs.

Alison was sitting alone in a rocking chair in the living room in the dark. As soon as she saw me she switched on a light. The soft glow of the lamp made her face seem really sad. I wished I'd had the courage to look her in the eye, but I decided to stare at the painting of the farmhouse on the wall behind her.

"Look, Alison. I know you've tried to be a good foster mother. And I sort of get why you kept that letter from me."

(Even though I didn't, not really.)

"You do?" she said, sounding pathetically hopeful.

"Sort of." I shrugged. "Anyway, I appreciate your offer to adopt me and everything. But I guess I'm pretty sure I don't want to—"

"Wait!" she cried, jumping up from the chair. "I've made a mistake. A horrible mistake. It was terribly self-ish of me, and I don't understand why I did it, except that I wanted to protect you. Please give yourself some time to think. You need time to gather all the facts. Things might look completely different in the morning."

Would they? Maybe, but I didn't want to wait to find out.

"No. I need to tell you now. I've changed my mind . . . about going to Alaska. If Mom's all better and if everyone says it's okay, then I'm going to tell the judge that that's what I want to do."

"Please, Ronnie. Don't be hasty. We can work things out, I know we can."

"No!" I shouted.

She looked surprised.

"Everyone said this was my decision. And right now my heart is telling me that Alaska, with my real family, is where I'm meant to be."

"But everything is in motion," she cried. "Your court date. The evaluations. Besides, your mother has big problems, Ronnie. You know that. The woman's not sta-ble. My goodness! After all she's done. How can you just throw away—"

"Because," I replied, angrily, "that *woman* you're talking about . . . just happens to be . . . my *mom*."

April 9

This morning I met with my Guardian ad Litem (GAL) in a wood-paneled office to tell her I was positive I wanted to live with my mother, so that at my court date she could advise the judge about what she thought was in my best interest. It's been almost a month since I read my mother's letter and I haven't changed my mind yet, so I guess that's saying something about the power of following your heart.

Francis took me to the meeting because Alison had patients and he happened to be free. Besides, Alison has been kind of cold and distant toward me ever since I told her about my decision. Or maybe I'm the one who's been cold to her—it's hard to tell. Anyway, I was glad I didn't have to sit with her all the way to Kutztown in the still-not-speaking-to-each-other silence of the car.

My guardian made me sign some papers on her metal desk, and advised me that I could still change my mind, but that after the court date in June there would be no turning back from my decision.

As we left the building, Francis opened his big black umbrella to shield us from the rain, and we ran through the wet parking lot to his car. We drove back on the highway in his blue Toyota Camry, which isn't half as much fun as his motorcycle, but necessary in the rain.

Francis asked me how Alison was doing. "Is she okay? She hasn't returned any of my calls." He seemed worried but also sad, like she could possibly be breaking his heart.

It wasn't like Alison not to return people's calls. Didn't she care about Francis, at least as a friend? Maybe she'd only been nice to him because of me. It made me feel angry that she would ignore him like that! I didn't know what to say to help him feel better, but a few minutes later I thought of the perfect thing.

"Alison's so controlling," I said. "No wonder she's gotten divorced two times. She'll probably never find anyone to love her."

It was still raining hard, and Francis's windshield wipers were on the fastest speed. "Ronnie!" he said angrily, "I find that extremely harsh!"

I stared out the blurry window and watched the cars go by.

"Lots of people love Alison. *You* loved her, didn't you?" he added.

"Maybe. I guess. Till she betrayed me. Now I *hate* her."

"*Hate* is not a word to be used casually." The bald spot on Francis's head darkened a shade. "You know, it's difficult for me to believe that you can so easily let your mother off the hook, but you can't seem to forgive poor Alison. I mean, what Alison did seems so *minuscule* in comparison."

What? I couldn't believe he was defending her!

"Minuscule?" I said. "Alison read my mother's letter! She tried to control my life by keeping it from me! That was *huge*! How can I ever forgive her for something like that?"

Francis pulled over to the side of the road, not even at a gas station or anything, and turned off the engine. A truck zoomed past us and splashed more water onto the windshield. We sat quietly together for a few minutes before he spoke again.

"Alison showed me that letter after we got back from dinner at the pub. She was very upset about it, naturally. She was fearful that you'd pick your mother over her . . . and that's exactly what's happened. Of course, it was wrong that she read it and that she kept it for so long, but everybody makes mistakes. She was hoping, in time, you might come to see. . . ." He paused, looking thoughtful.

"But she—"

"Wait a minute!" he said sharply. "Don't you realize how painful this must be for her, to have you living at her house, when she knows you might be leaving in June?"

"*Will* be leaving," I said, correcting him.

He shook his head. "Did it ever occur to you that she could say, 'Why don't you finish up at some other foster home?'"

What? "She would never do that!"

"Of course not. And do you know why? Because she won't abandon you. Not *ever.* Alison loves you. And although the judge will probably say you can go live with your mother, Alison continues to move forward with her plans for adoption. Not to control you, as you think, but so you'll have a back-up plan—just in case."

I glanced at him sideways. "In case what?"

He rubbed his hand over his bald spot and sighed. "Oh, Ronnie."

"You think my mom's going to screw up again, don't you?" I pounded my fist on the dashboard. "Well, she's not!"

"I didn't say that. And please don't hit my car. All I know is that Alison continues to go to meetings and court dates. She continues to cook your meals and wash your clothes and do all the regular things that she's always done for you, at least since you moved in with her last June. Look at all she's done for you! How can you say you hate her? What's *anyone* else done for you in the past three years that even comes close?"

I didn't have an answer.

Francis hesitated. "When is your next phone call . . . with your mom?"

"Next Friday, the day before my birthday. I talk to her like once a week now. Why?"

(During our last call, in fact, I had told her how excited I was about the upcoming spring dance. But that conversation hadn't gone very well.

"And it's in this really cool place, Mom, with a DJ and all these cute boys—"

"Boys? Well, you watch yourself, Ronnie. Don't let any of those boys get too close to you, okay?"

"What are you talking about, Mom?"

"I don't need you getting pregnant on me, Veronica Lynn! That's the last thing I need."

How she came up with something crazy like that, I have no idea, but it gave me a weird and creepy feeling.)

Francis was watching me closely. "I'd advise you to talk with her in depth," he said. "Ask her all sorts of questions. This is a very important decision. You need to think carefully about the life you might lead if you go to Alaska, because I believe it will be very different from the one you're leading here."

Whew. I was seriously upset after he finished that stupid lecture. "Can we please get going now?"

Francis started the car and pulled back onto the road. We drove home in silence except for the whir of the windshield wipers and the thudding sound of the rain.

When we got back to Alison's I told him thanks for the ride. He touched my arm and said *no problem.* "But please think about what I said. And tell Alison I said hello, okay?"

"Whatever," I said, shutting the car door. I jumped over a big puddle as I ran into the house.

Later today . . .

I called Cat to see if she wanted to sleep over because even if Paige found out, Cat is the only one who understands about me wanting to be with my mother. It felt weird to call her; I had pretty much dumped her months ago, but as soon as she came I could tell she didn't have any hard feelings, and we picked up right where we left off, which I guess is how it works with people who are meant to be your true friends.

At least that's how the night began, with the two of us doing our nails, sitting on my bed (just like old times) with my strawberry-scented candle flickering on the dresser. As I removed my old pink nail polish, I told her how I'd probably be living with my mother by summertime.

Cat was such a great listener, so much better than Paige. Why hadn't I ever noticed that before? "I'm so happy for you," she said. "See, it was worth waiting for!"

Then, as she was putting the clear polish top coat over her black fingernails, Cat asked if I could keep a really big secret.

I told her, of course, she could always trust me.

"You know how I've had a crush on Tyler Miller practically forever, right?"

(Along with half the girls in the school.)

"I guess."

She smiled coyly. "Well, now that Paige and he have officially broken up, do you think he'd go out with me?"

"Excuse me?" I said, trying hard not to laugh.

"I'm not joking," she said.

Had she seriously lost her mind?

While it was true that Paige and Tyler had broken

up last week (because Paige was way too jealous and controlling, according to Jon), the thought of Cat getting together with him was just plain crazy. Tyler was the most popular guy in school—and Cat was . . . well, it just wasn't going to happen.

Besides, the way these things usually worked, Paige and Tyler would probably be back together by tomorrow—or at least by some time next week, which is only one of the reasons why her idea was crazy.

"No offense," I said, "but they just broke up. I know she still likes him. And anyways, what makes you think you're his type?"

"Oh, *please*," she replied, like I was being so naive. "There are ways to get boys to like you." Cat began smiling the widest smile you could ever imagine, like she was secretly pleased about something, sort of like . . . well, a Cheshire cat.

And it got me thinking. Oh. My. God. Could that rumor about her be true?

"What's going on?"

She glanced at me with her guilty black eyes and then she quickly looked away.

"No way!" I said. "Please tell me you're not!"

"You worry too much," she said, leaning back on the pillow and blowing on her wet fingernails.

"But *you* don't worry enough! You always think they're going to like you—but they never do. And they especially won't if you start doing things like *that*!"

She just shrugged. "Maybe. Maybe not."

"What does that *mean*? What are you doing, Cat? How? When?"

But she refused to tell me any more, and a part of

me was glad, glad, glad, 'cause believe me, I'd rather not know. I tried to give her ten good reasons why she was worth so much more, that she was pretty and nice, and that she didn't have to resort to letting boys use her. Then I told her the most important reason of all.

"Seriously," I warned, "Paige would absolutely go ballistic if she ever found out you were with Tyler. You know she hates you. I mean, why would you want to make her even more of an enemy than she already is?"

Cat got quiet. "Maybe you're right. But, Ronnie, you're always telling me I should listen to my heart and that's all I'm trying to do. I've liked Tyler ever since fourth grade. And I would do just about anything to get him to like me back."

She looked so vulnerable lying there against my pillow; I just knew she was going to get hurt.

"I'm going to miss you when I move to Alaska," I said, feeling sad that I'd have to leave her behind.

"Me, too," she said. "Maybe I can visit when you get all settled?"

I agreed that would be awesome, but in the back of my mind I was thinking, where the heck would she even sleep in my mom's tiny apartment?

"It might take awhile," Cat said, "for us to get enough money to buy a ticket. Bud isn't working again, you know."

A part of me was afraid to ask, but I asked anyway. "So how are things going, you know . . . with *him*?"

"My mom's been around more, I guess."

I hoped that meant that Bud was leaving her alone.

Cat spent the rest of the night using her cell phone to call Tyler, or at least trying to call him, because every time she got through, his little brother would answer and see it was Cat (caller ID) and he'd hang up the phone, yelling, "Skank!" After a while she gave up and we watched a normal, boring, chick flick downstairs.

April 10

After Cat left this morning, I went into Alison's room and sat on her big, king-sized bed with its blue-and-white patchwork quilt and pretty throw pillows. She had just finished her shower and was trying to pull herself together, brushing her long hair in front of the mirror over her bureau, and putting on her earrings and makeup.

I decided to be nice for a change, remembering the conversation I'd had yesterday with Francis. I wanted her to know there were no hard feelings . . . on my part, anyway.

"Alison? I think I'm going to miss you when I move. Thanks for all you tried to do for me." She looked really pleased when I said that, so I went on.

"Remember that day when we rode to Allentown on the motorcycle?"

"I do." Alison smiled, and her eyes got all teary. "That sure was fun, wasn't it?"

"Yeah," I said. "It was the best day ever."

(I didn't have to make that up to help her feel better—it really was.)

I pulled my fingers through the soft fringe on one of the pillows. "Francis asked me yesterday if I knew why you hadn't called him lately. He said to say hello. I've been thinking—he might be good company for you. You know . . . after I'm gone."

Alison appeared troubled. "Oh dear, I've been meaning to call him." Her eyes met mine in the mirror over her dresser. "I'm afraid I haven't been very good company for anyone these days."

"*That's* for sure," I said, totally agreeing.

Maybe I'd agreed with her too quickly, because Alison's face got dark then, like she'd pulled down a window shade from the inside. She finished brushing her hair and clasped it in the back with a tortoiseshell barrette. "Listen, you don't have to worry about who is going to keep me company after you leave here, Ronnie. You've made your decision, and I'd appreciate it if you'd let me make mine."

I thought, so much for being nice to *her*, and went back to my room.

April 16 (the day before my birthday)

I was glad that my mom wasn't there today to see the expression on my face when I opened the package she sent for my birthday. Even Midge could tell it was inappropriate—an extra-small, pink sweater, with sequined hearts and kittens on it.

Kittens!

I'm not trying to sound ungrateful, but I would *never* wear something like that, not in a million years, even if it was the right size (which it wasn't), and it made me think, how well does my own mother even know me?

Still, Midge dialed the phone so I could thank her, since my birthday is on a Saturday and Midge's office will be closed. Mom asked me, did I get it, did I like it? Was I going to wear it to the dance tonight? When I tried to suggest that it just wasn't my taste, she got very annoyed.

"I hope that woman's not getting you used to things I can't afford!"

"You mean Alison? She's not. I just don't like it."

"Fine, then give it to one of your friends. Or better yet bring it up here so's we can return it. Just put it in your suitcase with the rest of your things."

"Okay," I said. Didn't she know that I never use suitcases?

Then she started telling me about all the fun we were going to have when I got to Alaska. Like going to see the glaciers. Riding snowmobiles. And the Iditarod races in the spring.

"All of those sled dogs, Ronnie! And I especially can't wait for you to meet Big Doug. I just know you're going to love him."

"Big Doug?"

"Didn't I tell you? I met him at an AA meeting. He's in recovery too. He used to do cocaine. He's gonna help us get another apartment."

He is?

"I thought Uncle Melvin was doing that."

"No, I used your uncle's money to get my car out of the shop. Doug's gonna move in with us. Or we'll move in with him. Not before you get here, of course. They won't let us. But Doug's cool with that. He'll wait till after those caseworkers split. We can't wait for them to get the hell out of our lives."

I couldn't help thinking, you mean the ones who are supposed to be looking out for me?

After a bunch of long silences she asked, "What's the matter *now*?"

"Are you sure that's such a good idea? Being with somebody who has the exact same problem as you?"

Mom snapped. "Keep out of my business, okay? I told you. He's in *re-cov-er-y*. I help him. He helps me.

154

We help each other out. I know *exactly* what I'm doing."

But obviously, my mother didn't have the best track record. Not with men. Not with men and drugs. And now she has this new boyfriend who used to be on drugs, and suddenly my head felt like it was going to split apart.

"You know, Mom, I've been thinking. I wonder if I should wait awhile . . . I mean before I come up there?"

"*Wait*? What for? Christ! You sound just like my frigging caseworker. I told you everything is going to work out. Are you changing your mind? You better not be changing your mind on me, Veronica! Not after all the hell I'm going through to get you back!"

Neither of us had much to say after that, so after some more long silences we hung up, still mad at each other, which has been happening ever since we've been allowed to talk more often to get us ready for "reunification."

Then, if that wasn't bad enough, after our call I had to sit through an hour of psychological testing, which was kind of hypnotizing, and I remembered stuff I hadn't thought about in years.

Alison had waited for me in the parking lot. It was sunny out, warm, springtime suddenly. Daffodils were beginning to bloom in the raised beds in front of the building. Alison had her window open and a book propped against the steering wheel.

When I got into her car, I slammed the door extra hard, slumped down in my seat, and said, "This totally sucks."

"Ronnie? What's going on?"

Should I tell her what had just happened? No, I decided to make up something instead.

"That stupid test took so much time! Now I'm going to have to rush to get ready for the dance!"

"Oh," said Alison, tossing the book she was reading into the backseat. "I thought it might have something to do with me."

I peered at her sideways. "What do you mean?"

"I'm sorry I've been so cold to you lately. Can't we please make the best of what little time we have left?"

"Sure, you've only been ignoring me for weeks!"

"You're right, but I'm only human, Ronnie. I needed time to sort out my feelings. I had planned to spend the rest of my life being your parent, and now I've got to let you go. I've talked it over with some of my friends and I'm feeling better now. I want to help make your transition go smoothly. Your happiness is still very important to me."

Before she put the keys into the ignition, she leaned over to give me a hug. I noticed that she smelled like that awesome perfume she always wears, a whiff of baby powder. Maybe she did care, I thought, at least a little bit. And our talk was so much better than the conversation I'd just had with my own mother that as we left the parking lot I felt sort of depressed . . . and very, very confused.

Later tonight . . .

Something really upsetting happened tonight at the dance. I don't even feel like writing about it, but if I don't get it out of my head, I know I'll never be able to fall asleep.

Alison drove the three of us (Paige, Britnee, and me) to The Factory, which is a converted warehouse-type teen center. It has a first floor with Ping-Pong tables and a snack room, and upstairs there's a dance floor and huge speakers—and they usually get a DJ who plays really good music. At every dance there's also about a dozen or so parent chaperones.

There was a loud rap song playing when we came in—it was vibrating all the windows downstairs. It was already crowded; everyone was there, at least half the school, because everyone just loves these dances.

First, we went into the bathroom to make sure we looked okay. We were all wearing our sexiest tops. I also wore my new low-rise jeans that Alison had bought me for my birthday, which I had talked her into letting me wear tonight.

Paige's halter was shimmering silver, mine was apple green, and Britnee had on a pale yellow tube top. After that we stood around at the snack bar, watching the door. Paige was looking for Tyler because she was hoping they would get back together tonight. We hung around downstairs to see if he would show up, but we didn't see him. So we squeezed our way through the crowded staircase and went upstairs.

Paige pulled on our hands to come dance with her because she just loved the song that was playing, called "Sex on the Beach," a loud, fun-to-dance-to song. But then it ended, and a slow song came on next. The reflecting ball hanging down from the ceiling made tiny dots of light all over the dance floor. There was a circle of kids in the middle of the room surrounding a couple who were slow-dancing. We walked over closer, making our way into the circle. The lights were dimmed, but it was easy to tell who the couple was.

Oh. My. God.

We just froze in our places and stared.

Cat was the girl in the center of the circle. She was

wearing this clingy red halter top (so tight, you could see *everything*) and she was grinding in a slow dance—with **Tyler**!

In case you don't know what grinding is, Tyler was standing behind her, up real close, and she had her backside to him and was rubbing herself against the front of his pants. He had this sly grin on his face, and he kept moving his hands along her hips. They seemed so comfortable with each other, it was like they were a couple or something, definitely more than just friends.

When I looked over at Paige, I could tell she was burning up with fury! She had been so sure that she would get back with Tyler tonight.

How had Cat done it? It didn't make sense.

Then I thought back to our conversation last week in my bedroom. Cat must be doing something with Tyler—it was the only logical explanation. But to go after someone's ex-boyfriend like that was the biggest insult of all time—so you can understand why Paige would be practically insane.

"Skank!" Paige screamed, but Cat didn't seem to hear. Maybe because her eyes were closed or the music was playing too loud—or maybe she was just too focused on her dancing.

Paige began waving her hands in front of her face, fanning herself. "Oh, my God, I can't breathe!"

It seemed like she was exaggerating, but we couldn't be sure. Britnee and I decided we'd better get her downstairs before she hyperventilated right in front of us. We pushed past all the dancing, jumping kids and hurried her down the staircase.

Britnee got some wet paper towels from the girls' bathroom, and we sat down on a couch by the door. Then, I guess because Paige wasn't getting enough attention sitting there, we went into the crowded room with the snack bar where the floor was sticky from spilled soda. "Do you want some bottled water?" I asked.

She said thanks and took a sip, while Britnee put a wet paper towel on the back of her neck.

"Jon told me boys have been going over to Cat's basement after school," said Britnee. "Like they've been taking turns."

"What! That is so gross," I said. This was way more serious than I'd thought.

"What am I going to do?" cried Paige. "I love him! I love him!"

Just as Paige began to settle down, Cat came into the room. Her round face was flushed from dancing, and her choppy hair was damp and clinging to her neck. She even had circular sweat stains under the arms of her red halter top. Disgusting! After she got her own bottle of cold water, she held it to her forehead. Then she leaned against a couch, and watched some of the seventh-grade boys playing Ping-Pong.

Cat didn't say hello to me because she'd learned, I guess, that if Paige was around I'd have to ignore her. But she did do something unexpected. You would think she'd be feeling guilty about how she'd just danced with Tyler, that she might slink away when she saw us—but instead she stared directly at Paige.

It was almost like a challenge.

"Look at her!" cried Paige. "I have to do something!"

Before we could stop her, Paige ran over and pushed at Cat's shoulder. "Why are you messing with my boyfriend?"

Paige's little shove meant nothing to big, old Cat; she barely moved.

"He's not your boyfriend anymore, right? You guys

broke up. Like two weeks ago."

Paige exploded. "You're gonna be so sorry, you whore! Everybody hates you!"

Cat's cheeks were flushed, but she kept her voice steady. "Not everybody hates me. Tyler sure doesn't. Why don't you go upstairs and ask him?"

With that, she tossed the empty water bottle into the garbage can, and began to walk through the doorway to the hall.

Paige's eyes narrowed. "You bitch!" she cried. She started to charge across the room, but we jumped up from the couch and held her back. The parent chaperones circled us, trying to find out what was going on.

Then some of the girls who had seen it gathered around Paige, saying things like, "You're so much prettier" and "We heard what she lets the boys do."

I didn't see Cat for the rest of the night because she went back up to the dance floor and most of the girls (at least all of Paige's friends) stayed downstairs. We couldn't stop talking about what had just happened and even the chaperones were trying to comfort Paige.

Around ten o'clock, when the dance was over, Britnee and I went outside into the parking lot to look for Alison's car. Even though tomorrow was the first day of spring break, the air felt freezing-cold since we'd been inside the warm building all night. Once we found her car, we had to search for Paige in the darkness, which wasn't easy because there were all these other kids running around looking for their rides too.

Finally, I spotted Paige and Tyler standing by the side of the building underneath a spotlight. Tyler was putting his arm around her, and she was crying into his tall shoulder. After they heard me call, he hugged her again, then they kissed in a way that was definitely *not* just friends. I felt sure they were getting back together, if not tonight, then tomorrow, or sometime really soon.

I also had this sinking feeling that things were going to get very, very bad.

For Cat, that is.

April 17—Early morning

Last night I had a very strange dream. I dreamed I was in Alaska running through the snow and I was searching for something. What it was, I didn't have a clue, but I had to hurry to find it. The snow was up to my knees, high enough that I kept sinking with every step. Since the snow was so deep, my boots slipped off and soon I was on my bare feet—still, I kept going. Eventually I found myself running toward the edge of this big, crystal blue body of water that was shaped like a bay, where jagged icebergs loomed in the distance.

And then there was my mother in a puffy red jacket, floating out to sea. She was sitting with her feet hanging off this gigantic iceberg (like in the movie *Titanic*) with Derek and Dan standing behind her. They were wearing red parkas too; bloodred, against the white snow.

They were floating away from me!

Wait! Wait! I tried to cry, but it was a dream so nothing came out of my mouth.

Even if they had heard me, I doubt they could have stopped.

And then I woke up.

Today is my birthday.

I'm fourteen years old.

April 17 (HAPPY BIRTHDAY TO ME!)

After I finished washing the breakfast dishes, Alison was going to take me to an acolyte meeting for church. She'd asked if I wanted to skip the meeting, since it was my birthday, and I wasn't going to be attending that church once I moved, but I told her no. "We're learning how to serve the Communion today. Besides," I said, "they obviously have churches in Alaska."

"Can I tell you again how sweet you looked last night?" Alison said, quickly changing the subject. "Did you have a good time?"

I'd felt so great wearing those new jeans she had bought me. "It was fun, I guess. You thought they fit okay?"

"Yes. Perfect. But I didn't like what Paige was saying on the way home. Who was she talking about anyway? Was it Cat?"

"I'm just going to have to destroy her," Paige had said in the car. *"She deserves it for all she's done."*

I hadn't told Alison anything about the whole Paige/Cat fiasco. Where would I even begin?

"I don't want to talk about it," I replied, wishing she wouldn't always listen in on my conversations.

"Okay," said Alison, putting her hand on my shoulder. "But remember, I'm always here if you ever do."

Then Alison reached into her purse and handed me a birthday card. On the front was a girl caterpillar changing into a butterfly. When I opened it there was a twenty-dollar bill inside. Alison had scribbled the words, *Happy Birthday. Keep the change.*

I smiled. "Ha. Ha. Very funny."

"You're not the same girl who moved in with me," she said wistfully. "You've made so much progress since then."

"Thanks." I put the money into my front pocket.

"Do you mind not having any other presents to open today?" She swept the crumbs from under the table into a dustpan.

"No, those jeans are awesome. Thanks again. Mom said we could celebrate when I get up there in June."

"Oh, yes, of course." I could tell Alison was trying not to sound too depressed. Two days ago, I'd found her sitting alone in my room on my bed, staring at the posters on my walls, like she was trying to memorize a part of me.

As I put away the dish towel, I glanced around the kitchen. I noticed the chocolate chip muffins in the bowl on the table, and the cut-glass vase full of white tulips near the sink. Alison always tried to make everything look so homey.

(Maybe I was trying to memorize a part of her, too.)

As we got ready to leave, she searched for her car keys in her purse. "Have you heard anything about your new school for next year?"

Midge had told me that Anchorage was a huge district with six high schools. It didn't seem quite real that I'd be going there in September.

"Mom still doesn't know which school yet. It all depends on where we move with Big Doug."

"Big Doug?" Alison asked, looking worried.

"My mother's new boyfriend." I shrugged. "Don't ask."

"Okay," she said, shaking her head. "But that reminds me. We received the date for your reunification hearing. June first. You'll only have two more weeks with me after that."

I glanced at the school calendar on her desk. April was almost over. I'd be here all of May, half of June, and

163

then I'd leave forever. I didn't know whether that thought made me feel happy anymore—or just worried and confused.

Alison dropped me off in front of church, where the training for the new acolytes was supposed to take place. I had grown to love this old, stone church, with its tall white steeple and beautiful stained-glass windows. I wondered what the churches would look like in Alaska. Before she pulled away, we both noticed Francis's motorcycle parked near the vestibule entrance.

"He certainly spends a lot of time here," said Alison. She said this in a way that seemed admiring and nice. "I hope you kids realize how lucky you are."

I knew I did, and then I remembered I'd soon be leaving Francis, too, and that thought made me feel sick inside, like when you suddenly see a "for sale" sign go up in front of the house of one of your best friends— except that the one who was going to be leaving . . . was *me*.

As I shut the car door, I decided that maybe I needed to skip that meeting after all. I went inside to look for Francis.

The door to the church office at the end of the hall was partway open. I found Francis sitting behind a big wooden desk, leafing through some papers. He was wearing the same pink tie-dyed shirt he'd worn to Puppy Kindergarten way back in the fall; so many things had happened since then.

I cleared my throat to let him know I was there. "Do you have a minute?"

Francis glanced up, took off his reading glasses, and

smiled. "For you, Ronnie? Always."

I sat down in the chair at the side of his desk and told him about how confused I'd been feeling lately. "It all started when my mother told me about her new boyfriend. I can't believe she's expecting me to move in with them. I don't even know him! Who has a stupid name like Big Doug, anyway?"

Francis frowned. "That does sound a little strange."

Then I described the dream I had last night, about trying to look for something and my family floating away from me. "Anyway, it was like a message," I explained. "Can dreams be messages?"

He rubbed his fingers on the top of his head like he does when he's listening hard. "What do you think it was trying to tell you?"

"That I need to change my mind? About going to Alaska? That I should stay here instead?"

Francis tried not to show it, but I knew that's what he thought I should do. "Perhaps," he said with a smile. "Would that be so terrible?"

I immediately felt all nervous and excited at the same time. "But they've already bought the plane ticket, and important people are making plans! Like the lawyers and the judge and the social workers and everything. I would feel so stupid changing my mind again."

"Not stupid; just the opposite. It's always better to stop, or at least pause, before heading down a certain path if you have significant doubts, rather than to proceed despite those feelings. I believe some people would call that *listening to your heart*."

I nodded. "The thing is—I'd really like to see my brothers again. I'm just not sure that I want to stay up there forever . . . you know . . . with *my mom*."

He looked me right in the eye. "I like how you're putting so much thought into this decision."

"Don't tell Alison, okay? I haven't told her because
I'm not positive. Not completely. Besides, no matter what
I decide, I just know somebody's going to get hurt."

He sighed. "There's no way around it. But Ronnie?
Let's try to make sure that that somebody doesn't end up
being *you*."

Francis let me sit on the couch in his office while he
finished up his paperwork. It felt calm and peaceful hearing the sounds of birds chirping outside his open window
and in the distance someone mowing their lawn. Then I
got up because it was almost time for the acolyte meeting
to be over, and I knew Alison would be outside waiting
for me in her car.

"Francis?" I stood in front of his desk again. "I want
to tell Alison about the day my mom left me, but I'm
afraid she'll use it against me somehow. Or try to influ-
ence my decision. You know, like she did before."

He put down his pen. "Tell her, Ronnie. You can trust
her. I believe Alison's learned a lesson from the last time."

"Learned my lesson about what?" said a voice from
behind me.

I spun around. It was Alison!

"Oh, I didn't mean to interrupt," she said, strolling
into the room. "What's this thing that you wanted to tell
me?"

It dawned on me that she must have been eaves-
dropping.

That made me so mad!

"How long have you been standing there?" I said,
glaring. "Listening to our *private* conversation?"

Alison seemed dumbfounded. "For crying out loud,

Ronnie, I just came in to get a drink of water. The door to the office was open. Why are you getting so—"

I turned to face Francis. "You actually expect me to trust *her*?" Then I pushed by her and stormed out of the room.

The curb next to her car wasn't the most comfortable place to sit. I leaned back on my elbows and tossed a few pebbles into the air. It had been ten minutes at least, but Alison still wasn't coming out. The church bells began ringing, which meant it was almost time for lunch.

I had calmed down since I'd come out here. Alison probably hadn't overheard much. Even if she had, what difference would it make? Mostly, I didn't feel like being angry at her anymore.

I went back into the church and was about to enter Francis's office when I heard voices coming from the other side of his door. I realized I could stand outside in the hallway, look through the crack in the door, and hear . . . *everything*.

"Anyway, thank you for taking the time to listen," Alison said. "I'm too close. She needs someone unbiased to help her sort things out."

(They were obviously talking about me.)

"Me? Unbiased?" Francis replied, laughing. "I'm not sure about that, but I try."

"I've avoided you lately," she said. "I'm sorry, it's just that—"

"I understand. This must be a very hard time for you."

Alison sounded like she was tearing up. "Yes, extremely difficult. It's taken me awhile to adjust to her decision. I still don't like it," she said. "But at least now, I think, I can accept it."

"I'm glad."

"Yes, it's been strange. Even with everything that's happened and how heart-wrenching it's been, I guess I'm just grateful that I've had Ronnie in my life at all."

Grateful?

I cracked open the door a bit more.

"'This is courage . . . to bear unflinchingly what heaven sends,'" Francis replied. "That's from a Greek poet, Euripides."

Alison smiled. "It's a lovely expression."

"Well, *you* look lovely today," he said. "You look wonderful, in fact."

"Why, thank you, sir," she said, sort of flirty. Then she walked across the room and kissed him quickly—right on the lips!

Francis seemed surprised and he was blushing, I think.

"Spring at last," he said, nodding toward his motorcycle helmet. "Perhaps I can talk you into another ride, Alison? Just you and me this time?"

Was he asking her out on a date?!

"I'd love that," she said as they walked toward the door.

Suddenly Alison stopped.

"Francis, wait," she said, taking hold of his hand. "I want you to know . . . you've made all the difference. Ronnie trusts you. I don't know what she . . . what *we* . . . would have done without you."

He smiled and shook his head. "She may trust me, Alison, but it's *you* that she loves."

"Do you really think so?" Alison asked, her eyes tearing up.

I nodded to myself because I realized that what he was saying was completely true.

"I know she does," he answered. "But she's not the only one."

I should have left them alone to enjoy their private moment, yet I couldn't tear myself away. Francis put his arm around Alison and pulled her in close. They started kissing! It was a long, romantic kiss! After they'd finished, they looked into each other's eyes, not saying a word.

(Maybe there were no words to describe how they were feeling.)

When I opened the door, they looked mildly surprised to see me, but they didn't stop hugging or gazing at each other or smiling—it was like, how can I explain it?

They laughed and pulled me into their arms, saying, "Come here, *you!*"

And it all felt so perfectly right. Like the three of us had finally come home.

April 25

This is the biggest decision I've ever had to make. I can't mess up. So why is it that one minute I'm so sure I want to stay with Alison and the next . . . ?

I keep looking for a sign to tell me what to do, but I'm not picking up *anything*. Why has God *completely* deserted me just when I need him the most? My court date is only five weeks away!

It's all I've been able to think about this whole spring vacation, and besides sleeping late and walking Lucky and watching TV, I can't seem to think about anything else. I'm so glad I have school tomorrow, because school always distracts me.

Francis thinks I'm having a "dark night of the soul." He explained that this is what happens when you are forced to confront your own demons.

He asked me this morning after church what is preventing me from deciding on Alison, because truly, most of the time, I'm ninety-nine percent sure I want to stay with her. "What are you afraid of happening if you stay here?"

"I still don't completely trust Alison. She kept that letter from me. What if she turns around and does something like that again?"

"There's a clue for you in there somewhere," he said.

So, I thought and thought about it, but all I could come up with was that for some reason it reminded me of when my mom left with Kenny, and how she chose him over me, and how I never want to go through that again. What if I do something to make Alison really mad and she decides to kick me out the door? I don't have the best track record when it comes to my bad behavior. How do I know I won't make another mistake?

This morning the sermon was about how to forgive those who have betrayed us, like Peter in the garden and all of that stuff. It got me wondering if maybe this was the sign I'd been looking for, if God was trying to tell me something. And if it was, what did it mean? Who did I need to forgive most?

My mom for leaving me?

Or Alison for the letter?

And what could I do to make sure that whoever I picked would never, *ever* leave me again?

When I asked Francis he said, "You didn't do anything that made your mother leave you. It wasn't your fault, Ronnie. You know, maybe it's not your mom or Alison who you need to forgive most. Maybe you just need to forgive yourself."

April 30

So now I want to write about what happened to Cat this past week at school, because there is so much to tell. Although Cat did something really stupid, there's no way she deserved all the things that were done to her.

Tyler and Paige had made up over spring break, just as I predicted. They were back together again, all lovey-dovey, the "perfect" couple. I had even seen them holding hands together at the mall when I was shopping with Alison.

A few days ago, on the first Monday after vacation, Paige said she had a plan to make Cat's life completely miserable (as if it weren't already miserable enough). She told us she was going to make damn sure that whatever happened between Cat and Tyler never happened again.

Cat had her usual Monday migraine, so she missed the whole conversation (not that Paige would ever let her hear it), but I had to sit there on the crowded bus and listen to Paige plot and plan her revenge. It made me feel sick, but what could I do? I was Paige's best friend; I had to support her.

I will get to all she did to Cat in a minute, but first I have to say that it amazed me that Paige wasn't mad at Tyler AT ALL and had managed to fix all the blame on Cat. Like Tyler was helpless, merely a "victim," like he had nothing to do with "it" happening.

What was up with that?

Obviously he was at least *half* to blame, but I would never say that to Paige. I guess that makes me a terrible chicken—or perhaps very, very smart.

Paige's cruelty knew no limits, and she got the entire school to help her administer the torture. Here's a Bible verse that sums it all up in one sentence:

The tongue has the power of life and death.
(Proverbs 18:21)

On Tuesday, in math, Mr. Sorenson asked Cat to come to the front of the class to do a problem. I sat directly behind her, with Jon on the left (next to me). As she walked up to the board in her black sweatshirt and sweatpants, I saw Jon pull something out of his pocket and sneak a quick look around. Then he took a condom(!)—pale yellow, long, and thin—and stuck it to the outside of Cat's notebook, which was sitting on her desk.

(I knew that's what it was because I'd seen condoms before—in health class and on TV.)

When Cat returned to her seat, she noticed it right away. She turned around quickly and whispered, "Ronnie. Oh. God. Who put this here?"

"How should I know?" I replied, feeling terrible, and then I opened my book and pretended to be doing a problem.

Jon leaned across his desk with a sly grin on his face. "You left that at my house," he said to her, loud enough for anyone around us to hear.

Cat put a fist to her mouth, slammed her notebook on the floor, and ran out of the room. In between classes it got worse.

Kids lined up in the hallways, waiting for her. As Cat walked along, minding her own business and trying to get to class, they hissed out the words, "Slut! Ho! Bitch!" Rotten things like that. It was awful.

Cat's head would whip around fast, but the kids were sneaky and would lean casually against the wall so she couldn't be sure who said it and so none of the teachers would get suspicious.

I knew what they were doing was wrong, but my feelings were all jumbled up inside. I didn't need this kind of stress right now! Mostly I tried to avoid hallways where I thought she might be, or I lagged behind if she was in front of me.

"Gross!" some boys would say, right to her face, or "Ugly," when they bumped into her or blocked her way.

During lunch on Wednesday, they shot spitballs at her while she was sitting (all alone) eating her sandwich. Some kids just spit as they walked by with their trays. A boy named Brian McPherson stuck gum in her hair.

None of the lunch aides noticed a thing!

On Thursday after lunch they put some kind of crap—dog crap or human crap(!)— into the bottom of her locker. How disgusting is that? The smell was penetrating; it was a warm spring afternoon. The odor spilled into the hallway so that people had to hold their noses when they passed.

"What am I supposed to do with this, Ronnie?" she asked when she found it at the end of the day. Her eyes filled with tears.

I shrugged. "Maybe you can ask the janitor to clean it up?"

The worst was yet to come.

Today, Friday, I was standing just inside the door-way for study hall, when Tyler and some of his friends, Jon included, cruised slowly by. They were all tall and lanky, with baseball hats turned around on their heads. Cat was getting a drink at the water fountain that had been clogged for the entire year. Tyler was laughing as he came down the hall, with his slit eyes right on her.

Jon started talking really loud on purpose. "Hey, tell us the truth. Do you miss her, Tyler?"

"Miss who? You mean *Cat?*" said Tyler, making sure she heard him.

For a brief second she looked desperately hopeful.

"You went over to her basement, right?" said Jon.

"So did you!"

"Shut up, man. How was she?"

"Well, if I had to grade it," Tyler said, laughing, "I'd probably only give her a C minus—no wait—I think she was a D."

Then they all laughed. Like a bunch of insane idiots. Cat looked like she wished she could completely disappear. How could they be so cruel? I watched as what little was left of her self-esteem slowly drained out of her body.

May 18

Lately, Cat hasn't been showing up at school. Big surprise, huh? She's missed lots and lots of school. She's been absent every day for the past two weeks.

You have to give her credit, though; she tried to keep coming back, but then I guess she couldn't stand it anymore. For her, just getting down the hallways must have been like being a death row prisoner on the way to the electric chair—which might make you wonder, why didn't any of the adults try to stop it?

That's easy. Cat didn't tell them. I suppose she didn't want anything she'd done with those boys to come out to her family. After all, she'd had plenty of experience with adults either not believing her or doing nothing whatsoever to help. As far as I know, she kept her mouth shut the entire time.

And so did everybody else.

The last time I saw her was almost two weeks ago, when she stepped off the school bus at our stop for the last time. She was shuffling along slowly with her eyes on the ground, and I thought to myself, this is what somebody looks like when they've been *obliterated*.

May 21

Okay, so maybe I'm a little jealous that Francis and Alison are now an "item," as she likes to call their new dating situation, because, frankly, it's taking a lot of time away from me. Tonight I found her upstairs in her robe after her shower instead of in the kitchen making my dinner. She had three possible outfits laid out on her bed and she was in a panic over what to wear. *Please.* Like Francis would ever expect her to look perfect.

"But tonight's different," she explained. "He's taking me someplace special to celebrate our anniversary."

"Really?"

"One month exactly. On Tuesday."

I thought, oh, that is just so lame.

"Do you think this is dressy enough?" She held a purple skirt up to the mirror. "Or will it make me look old and frumpy?"

I made a face. "What are you freaking out about? It doesn't matter."

"It matters," she said, getting annoyed, "to *me*."

Obviously she didn't actually want my opinion, so I gave up and went downstairs.

About half an hour later she came down dressed all nice and smelling pretty. I was sitting on the beanbag chair with Lucky curled up next to me. I had a can of Coke in my hand and was eating a bag of Utz potato chips. (Dinner, I guess.)

She tried to chat for a few minutes before she left for the evening (probably so she wouldn't feel guilty), but I responded with one-word answers.

"Don't forget you can have that leftover chili for supper," she said. "It's in the fridge."

"Okay."

"We'll call to check in with you when we get there."

"Sure."

"You're awfully quiet tonight," Alison said, looking at me strangely.

"*So?*" I picked up the TV remote and began scanning.

"Is it because Francis and I are going out without you?"

"*Please.*"

"You know he has that motorcycle trip coming up. We just wanted to spend some time together. He'll be gone for a whole week."

"I'm not upset."

But when I turned to look at her, I surprised both of us, I guess, by a single tear beginning to slide down my face.

Her cell phone rang before she could say anything

more. I could tell by the tone of her voice that it was Francis. She went into the bathroom, where she now goes for their private calls, and then, unexpectedly, she came right out again.

Alison sat down across from me on the soft, velvety couch. I was still curled up on the floor. "That was Francis. He had to cancel." She patted her leg and smiled. "So come. Sit right up here and tell me."

"I'm too big. I'll hurt you."

"No, you won't. Come here. I know something's wrong. Talk to me, please."

She pulled me out of the beanbag chair and sort of folded me into an arrangement on her lap.

I tucked in a tag from her new blouse that was sticking out. Suddenly I felt awful for ruining their evening. "Did he really have to cancel? Or are you just saying that? I don't want to wreck your plans."

She smiled sympathetically. "It's okay. The restaurant lost our reservation. We couldn't get in anywhere this late anyway. Besides, you won't be with me much longer. Francis and I can go out anytime."

I didn't completely believe her, but felt relieved just the same. I took a deep breath. "Maybe now is a good time to tell you about the day my mother left me."

"Okay." Alison seemed excited. Her eyes lit up with anticipation.

"Relax," I said. "This isn't a miracle breakthrough or anything—just something I'm finally ready to tell you."

"Of course, dear." Alison sighed. "I promise to listen all the way through." She began rubbing my shoulders, and I snuggled into her lap, just like she was the warm, comfy sofa I'd always imagined her to be. Then I told her what I remembered.

It was moving day. Two weeks before my birthday. Kenny was out getting supplies for the long trip across country. Mom had to pick up her paycheck, so I was told to do the last-minute packing. She was running around like crazy, barking orders.

"Whatever you can fit in one Hefty bag, that's all you can bring from your room. And help your brothers with their toys. Kenny said we can't take all their shit, so just pick out something they'd miss if it got left behind."

She gave us lunch—Subway from the corner— and then she left.

The TV was packed away, so I played with the boys for an hour or so, making up games with the left-over boxes. Then I took down some posters from my room and cleared off my dresser, stuffing the plastic bag until it couldn't hold another thing.

The afternoon went by slowly. Danny kept pulling toys out of his bag, and I had to keep repacking it. Around dinnertime they were getting cranky and hungry. I managed to find a box of macaroni and cheese in the cabinet, and I put it into a bowl with some water and heated it in the microwave for a snack. After we finished eating, Derek and I played a game of hangman with some of his spelling words from school.

Finally I heard the rumble of the truck as it pulled into the parking lot in front of our apartment. I looked out the living-room window. They were sitting in the front seat. Kenny was waving his arms around and Mom was shrinking away from him—like maybe they were having a fight.

I lugged my heavy bag outside and stood on the

cement stoop, figuring that might get them to stop arguing. My mother got out of the U-Haul, but Kenny stayed behind the steering wheel. When she came closer, I noticed she had a bruise on her cheek—and she'd been crying.

"What took you so long, Mom?"

I knew not to mention the mark on her face.

"It's a big deal, Ronnie, moving this far away. We had lots of things to take care of."

All of a sudden Kenny leaned on the horn—three long blasts. "Hurry the hell up!" he yelled out the window.

"This is important," she screamed back at him. "Give me a minute, Christ!"

And that's when she told me.

"Ronnie, I need you to listen. We can't take you with us. There's not enough room. I tried to work it out with Kenny, but we're driving all the way cross-country. There's only room for us and the boys. You need to stay behind with Uncle Melvin and Raylene. Just until we get settled. I left a message for them to pick you up as soon as they get home from that church trip they're on. Don't open the door till they get here, okay? Just wait for Uncle Mel."

For some reason, I didn't even try to argue with her.

Maybe I was in a state of shock.

"I promise we'll send for you soon," she said. "As soon as we save enough money for a plane ticket."

Then I got excited. "So I'll have my birthday party in Alaska?"

The guilty look on her face told me all that I needed to know.

"Not this year. Try to make the best of it, Ronnie. Okay?"

The boys tumbled out the front door with little Danny yelling, "Go now, go." But Derek must have realized something was wrong as she pushed them along the sidewalk toward the truck.

"What about Sis?" Derek cried. He ran back to where I'd been left standing. "We're not leaving without Sis!" he insisted, and Dan, toddling along, started whining too. I tried to hold back my tears.

"Give her another hug, boys. Sis will be fine."

My mother picked up Dan under her arm, and put the two boys in the backseat, then she came back to get their toys. She handed me a pillow, but she wouldn't meet my eyes. "You can do this for me, Veronica, right?"

I felt like I'd been kicked in the face.

I stood there, with the pillow in my arms and my bag next to me, as Kenny backed the truck out of the parking lot. I remember hoping and praying that this was just their way of teaching me a lesson, that any second they'd come peeling back around the corner, saying okay, you can come with us, if you promise to be good from now on. But of course that didn't happen. After about an hour, I went into the empty apartment, rested my head on my pillow, and waited for my uncle to come get me.

Alison was quiet, not sure I had finished.

"That's about it," I told her.

"How incredibly sad. You must have felt so alone."

I shrugged. "I guess. But I know kids who have had it much worse."

I was thinking of the other kids I'd met in foster care. Like Jeremy, whose mother burned his fingers with hot candle wax; and Amanda, who watched her dad stab her mom to death; and Carly and Crystal, who had to sleep in a cage.

And then there was Cat, who hadn't even been in foster care, but had been through a hell of another kind.

"Don't minimize your situation. It sounds awful!" Alison gave me a hug. "So you spent that first night at your uncle's house?"

"No. They picked me up the next day. Around lunch time, I guess."

Alison seemed very upset. "The next *day*? You mean to tell me that after your mother announced she was abandoning you that you had to stay there—in that empty apartment, *all night long*? I'm sorry, Ronnie, but what kind of mother would *do* something like that?"

My mother, I thought.

I shrugged off the memory. "Don't hate her, Alison, please. My mom is weak. She's always been weak. Kenny must have beaten her; that's why she left me."

Alison gave me another hug. "I don't hate her, honey. It just makes me feel sad."

I remembered the expression on my mother's face right before she left me: afraid, guilty, defeated. "I feel sorry for her too."

Alison blinked. "What? No. What I meant was that your mother was an adult. You were only a child. No matter what Kenny did to her, your mother still had choices—she just couldn't see her way to making the right one. No, Ronnie, I feel awfully sad for *you*."

"Oh."

I snuggled back into her warm shoulder and felt her arms wrap all the way around me. I suddenly knew that no matter what happened, Alison, *my* Alison, would *always* choose me.

May 26

The guidance counselor gave me Cat's schoolwork to take home to her today so her tutor wouldn't have to pick it up. The school had arranged for her to be on home study for medical reasons (incapacitating migraines and colitis brought on by stress). There were only a few weeks left of school, anyway.

So this afternoon, I went over to her house. I noticed the shrubs in front of her driveway needed clipping, and old newspapers were collecting like dog bones on either side of her front porch. I was carrying her math workbook, last week's assignments, and the rubric for our history project.

When she answered the door, Cat looked sickly and tired. Her white skin was paler than ever. The brown roots at her part-line were about three inches grown into her blue-black hair, and she was wearing long sloppy sweatpants and a sweatshirt, even though it was hot and steamy outside.

She asked me to come inside, and I told her okay, but only for a few minutes. I felt sorry for her, but after all that had happened, it also felt strange, like we didn't really know each other anymore.

We went into her family room, and I swept some of the old magazines off the couch so I could sit down and explain the homework. Her dog, King, was asleep on the rug. I opened our history book and handed her the outline from our teacher.

"Now here's what you have to do."

"Don't bother," she said, tossing the outline on the table. "I don't have the energy. Sometimes I wish I was dead."

What? Why was she talking that way? It gave me a creepy feeling.

"Let me show you, please," I said, pointing to example one. "It's easy."

"No, I want to show *you* something instead."

She held out her arm and carefully rolled up her sleeve. There were a dozen cut marks on the inside of her arm! These cuts were much worse than the few surface scratches from before—they were raw and red and deep. She also pulled up a leg of her sweatpants— ragged cuts, pink and infected, circled the bottom half of her shin. Around the bone of her ankle she had carved the word **RAGE**.

Seeing those cuts made me realize how far I had come in getting better, and I thanked God I had never gotten that bad. But it also made me realize how much trouble Cat was in. How sick she'd become. Did anyone else know about this? It scared me.

"Oh my God, Cat. That is *so* not cool!"

"I guess. But you don't know what it's been like for me."

"What do you mean? With Bud?"

She hesitated.

"Bud's the reason, isn't it? Why you were with all of those boys?"

"He's not bothering me anymore," she replied angrily. "I told him I'd shoot his balls off in his sleep if he ever touched me again."

It seemed like she meant it too.

"But he's the reason you've been cutting yourself, right?"

Her eyes narrowed. "What are you talking about, Ronnie? I just told you I took care of that. It's *school.* Hello? Were you blind? Didn't you see what those kids were doing to me? I was *completely* alone there. My mother says I have to go back, but I can't go back to school. Not ever."

I thought about all the things Paige and the others had done to her and suddenly I felt unbelievably guilty and sad. She was right. She had been alone.

Why hadn't I tried to help her? Why hadn't I walked next to her as she walked down those hallways of doom, or sat at her table when she was being tortured at lunch? I could have approached Paige and tried to get her to stop. (Not that it would've done any good . . . but still.) There's a chance I could've convinced some of the other kids to come over to Cat's side.

But I hadn't done any of those things. None of us had. We had all been too weak and caught up in it, and ultimately, I guess, we didn't want the same thing to happen to us. I had betrayed Cat once again. And what was worse, I realized, I was equally to blame: for simply looking the other way.

"Oh, Cat, I am so sorry." I stared at the wounds on her leg again, which were practically shouting at me from near the bottom of her pants. "But you can't cut yourself anymore," I said. "We can talk to Alison. She can find somebody to help you. Like a therapist or something. Maybe you can even change schools."

The late afternoon sun streamed through a crack in the curtains of her family room. Cat looked defeated. "A therapist isn't going to help me get my reputation back," she answered, shaking her head. "It's gone forever. And my mother can't afford to send me to another school."

"Well, maybe it'll be different next year in high school. Like a whole new fresh start."

But even I didn't believe that—and seeing her face, I knew Cat didn't believe it either. "How will it be different, Ronnie? Paige will still be there, right? Tyler? Jon? What's going to change?"

She had a point. It was hopeless. Even King, who had curled up beside her, put his head down at her feet and sighed.

"Paige really is a bad person," she added. "I mean she's truly evil, Ronnie. She'll never let me forget what I did."

(I was beginning to come to the same conclusion.)

She pulled a pillow from behind her and punched it hard. "I wish I could teach her a lesson."

There was suddenly a flicker of hope in her nearly empty eyes. "What if I got Paige over here somehow," she suggested. "In my basement, and I don't know . . . scared her somehow? Maybe if I told her I'd hurt her if she didn't knock it off, then she'd tell everybody to stop. She can control them, you know. Maybe if she agreed to stop it, then I could go back to school. Not this year, obviously—this year is pretty much over. But next year. A fresh start, Ronnie, like you said."

For the first time that afternoon, she looked almost like her old self. But I felt nervous. Unsure.

"I don't know, Cat. I don't think it would work. I mean how would you scare her? You wouldn't hurt her or anything, would you?"

"Are you serious?"

"Okay. Then what would you do?"

It might have only been the afternoon light penetrating the room, but her eyes seemed to take on a sudden strange and eerie glow. "You could help me, Ronnie," she said, smiling for the first time in like *forever*. "After all that's happened, I think you kind of owe me. I've been sitting here for days. I've had lots of time to work this out—and I think I have a plan."

May 27

Here was the first part of the plan: I had to tell Paige that Tyler was still meeting Cat in her basement after school. Why Paige would believe that Cat would continue doing something like that after all the torture Paige had put her through was beyond me, but Cat said, "Trust me, Ronnie. She will." She refused to tell me how she was planning to scare Paige, but, knowing Cat, I figured it probably wouldn't be so bad.

So the next day, during the cool, early morning of first period, I approached Paige in gym class. We were sitting outside on the damp bleachers at the tennis courts waiting for our turn to play. Paige loved to play tennis, and was by far the best player in the whole eighth grade. It was hard for me to get her attention because she kept following the action on the courts.

"Listen," I finally said, gripping her arm, "this is

extremely important. . . ."

As she looked into my eyes, I told her the lie about Cat and Tyler.

"No way," said Paige, shaking her head. "I don't believe it. Tyler text-messaged me last night—he *loves* me. He's always telling me that he loves me. She's just saying that to try to break us up."

I had sort of expected Paige to be more suspicious of Tyler, but Cat had warned me to be prepared. *"Improvise, Ronnie, if necessary."*

One of the girls hit a ball over the fence near where we were sitting. Paige got up, threw it back, and sat back down again.

"He said I could trust him, Ronnie. And I do, *most* of the time. . . ."

"But what if Cat is telling the truth?" I asked. "I mean that would be awful, right? What if you could find out for sure? Wouldn't you want to know?"

"I guess so." She looked tense. "Of course."

A big puffy cloud covered up the sun temporarily. I zipped up my jacket and pulled it over my knees.

"What if we could sneak into her house?" I suggested. "Her family always leaves the front door unlocked. What if we could catch the two of them in the act?"

"I don't know," she said, examining a broken fingernail. "When?"

"What about today after school?"

Paige's lips were turned downward, not yet convinced. "Tyler has tutoring today, I think."

(Cat already knew this since they have the same tutor.)

"Well, she started bragging about how he's going

straight to her house today—*after* tutoring. But if he's not in her basement when we get there, then we can always bitch her out for spreading rumors. Either way you win, right?"

Paige nodded, half sure. The sun returned, shining on both of our faces; it was going to be a warm, beautiful day. "You would definitely come with me?"

"No problem. Don't tell anyone, though," I added cautiously. "Not even Britnee. 'Cause if Tyler finds out then they might just decide to meet some other time, and then you'll never know for sure."

Paige sat there for a long minute, turning it over in her head.

"Okaaay," she said slowly. "But why is she telling you all this stuff, anyway? It makes me wonder if the two of you are still friends."

"*Please*," I said, putting my arm around her shoulders. "I have no idea why she's telling me—she caught me online last night. But if I had to pick between you and Cat, isn't it obvious by now which one of you I'd choose?"

Paige smiled her beautiful, perfect smile. "Okay, let's do it."

She fell for it. I couldn't believe it!

Step one of Cat's plan was on its way.

Later today . . .

Here's what happened.

I must have looked at the clock in language arts at least a thousand times before it finally said 2:15. Paige got off the bus with me after school and we walked to my house. We watched TV, waiting until we knew Tyler would be done with tutoring. After we had a Diet Coke and I let Lucky out to do his business, we left for Cat's.

As I closed our front door, I noticed that it had become one of those fantastically hot days in late spring, when you can almost smell the scent of coconut suntan lotion in the air. I realized I could be working on my tan right now instead of being part of this crazy scheme. But there was no turning back. We walked the two blocks to Cat's house, pausing at the mailbox at the end of her walk. With the curtains drawn and the lawn unmowed, the shabby house seemed almost deserted.

Step two was almost here.

Paige seemed nervous. "Is anyone home? Like her mom or something?"

"I'll check and see."

I peeked in the garage window first: no cars. Cat had told me her mom and Bud would be working, but to check just to make doubly sure. The front door was unlocked, as usual. King barked twice when we came in, but he knew me—so he hopped onto the couch and left us alone. I led Paige through Cat's messy house, which felt odd since there was no one around.

As we walked by a few bulging plastic garbage bags in the hallway outside the kitchen, Paige wrinkled up her nose and brushed pretend dirt off her arms. "*Somebody* doesn't have a cleaning lady."

Why did she have to be so mean?

I took her over to the basement door. "Here it is," I said, reaching for the handle.

But when I tried to pull it open, it wouldn't budge, and that got me thinking, what if this isn't such a good idea after all?

"It's stuck," I announced. "Why don't we come back some other time?"

"I don't *think* so." Paige pushed me out of the

way and tugged the door hard, almost falling when it suddenly came free. She smoothed her hair and began to march down the stairs. I took a deep breath and followed right behind her.

The basement was dark and musty-smelling. I called out, "Cat?" just like I was supposed to.

Paige whispered, "Shut up, stupid! Do you want her to hear us?"

"Ronnie?" Cat answered, but we still couldn't see her. "Go away! We're kinda busy right now. I told you Tyler was coming over!"

Paige turned around to look at me with her mouth wide open in total shock.

I began to walk backward up the stairs.

Paige looked angry. "What the hell, Ronnie? Are you bailing on me?"

"Don't worry," I said calmly. "I'm just going to turn on the light."

This was the second part of the plan. Cat said I had to leave them down there alone. I hurried up the rest of the stairs, flicked on the light, and then I shut and locked the door behind me. I ran as fast as I could past King on the couch, past the garbage bags in the hallway, and out the front door to the stoop.

I was supposed to come back and let them out in around half an hour—to give Cat enough time to do whatever it was she had decided to do. *Trust me, Ronnie. I swear. Just enough to scare her.*

Paige deserved to be taught a lesson, right? The way she'd tormented Cat, I didn't have any other choice but to go along. But as I stood there near the unkempt shrubs of Cat's nearly deserted house, I was overcome by a weird sort of feeling. After the dark of Cat's basement, the sun seemed almost too bright outside. A robin with a twig in its mouth was perched on the mailbox. Everything looked normal, ordinary. Except that it wasn't. Everything was all mixed up. I needed time to think.

Paige had done some pretty horrible things to Cat, so she deserved to be punished—but what if Cat planned to do something equally horrible in return? I pictured those cuts she'd made on her arms and legs. What if Cat wasn't being completely honest with me? *"Remember, Ronnie, not telling the whole truth is also lying,"* Alison had said.

What if Cat was thinking about hurting Paige?

I glanced at my watch. It had only been a few minutes since I'd left them, but my heart was beating out the words:

Go back.

Go back in.

Go back inside.

Everything was quiet inside the house. As I walked through the living room, King lifted his tired old head from the couch and then put it back down again. I quickly went past the same dirty glasses on the coffee table, the same piles of garbage in the hallway, and hurried over to the basement door.

I tried the door handle. The door was still locked. So I unlocked it, tugged it open, and called downstairs. "Cat?"

Nothing.

Only creepy black darkness, except for one dim lightbulb hanging by a string.

"Paige?" I called.

There was a rustling sound of someone moving.

"Ronnie?" It was Paige's voice.

"Yeah?"

"Help me, Ronnie! Get down here, quick!"

She sounded terrified. And that's when I got really scared.

I ran down those basement steps, two steps at a time, absolutely dreading what I might find. When I got to the bottom, I peered around the back of the staircase. That's where I found them. At first they looked almost normal—except for the way they weren't moving, and the horrible look on Paige's face, and the fact that Paige was crouched on the floor and Cat was standing across from her, frozen in a way that seemed like she was playing some kind of pantomime game.

And then I saw it. I don't know how I'd missed it.

It was as if my worst fear had come true.

Cat was holding a *gun*!

She began waving it around as I watched her. There was this dazed sort of look on her face, like she wasn't totally there, like she didn't even see me.

I could feel my heart thudding and there was a rushing sound in my ears.

Paige was on her knees, trying to protect her head with the crook of her elbow. "Oh my God, Ronnie! What's she going to do?"

Just then, the angle of the setting afternoon sun penetrated one of the basement windows. I glanced at it for just a second, but then, while my eyes readjusted to the darkness, it seemed like things were happening in slow motion, but speeding up at the same time.

I looked over at them again.

Cat had put both hands on the gun and was now aiming it at Paige.

Paige was crying, whimpering a helpless sort of moan.

I knew I had to do something—*fast*.

"No, Cat, *STOP!*" I screamed as loud as I could. She glared at me, and her arm jerked back. Then I heard a loud noise, like a pop!

I covered my face with my hands.

When I peeked through my fingers, I saw Paige checking herself—patting her arms and legs, as if she couldn't believe Cat had missed her. Then she jumped up and flew past me up the stairs.

"Get out of here, Ronnie, she's crazy!"

I'd never seen anyone run that fast.

Cat stood there, motionless, her hand by her side, looking stunned.

And that's when I started screaming. At first I thought it was Cat who was screaming, but it wasn't her, it was me.

"You tried to shoot her!" I screamed, again and again.

"The gun's never loaded," she explained in a monotone, almost like she was trying to convince herself.

"But you pulled the trigger!" I cried. "Why did you do that?"

Cat shook her head. "It was an accident, I swear! You've got to believe me. I just wanted to teach her a lesson—to scare her—that's all. She was calling me horrible names, a liar. A whore. I hate her! I hate all of them for that!"

"You can't go around shooting at people just because you hate them!"

"But I told you the gun's never—"

"Fine, Cat. Try telling that to the police, which—by the way—Paige is probably calling them this very second! They put kids in jail for stuff like this!"

Cat's eyes filled. "You're right. Oh my God. I'd rather die than rot in jail."

It seemed like she meant it too. I realized she might be feeling desperate.

"Listen, Cat. Maybe you won't have to . . . go to jail, I mean . . . you didn't hurt her, okay? It was an accident. You didn't know the gun was loaded."

"What? No, you were right the first time. I'd better be going now."

At first I thought she was planning to run away, which probably to her made a whole lot of sense. But then I saw the way she was holding the gun up near her head, and I was afraid she might actually try to do something crazy. Like shoot herself!

"Come on. Don't do anything stupid, okay?"

Her eyes went blank. "No. For once I'm thinking of doing something really smart."

Oh my God! How was I going to stop her?

"Don't, Cat, please. Just give me the gun. You won't go to jail, I promise. I'll take all the blame. I'll tell them it was completely my idea, all my fault, that I planned everything."

"You would do that for me?" she said, her bottom lip quivering.

I realized by this point that we were both going to be in huge trouble, no matter which one of us took the blame. I was going to lose everything!

Everything because of this!

"Why not? Alison won't keep me when she finds out my part. My mom won't want me either. I'll be sent away for sure. Come on, just give it to me."

She hesitated. I moved a little closer. It was almost in my reach.

Tears began pouring down her face. "But, Ronnie," she sobbed, "how do I know I can trust you?"

I smiled. "Remember? Like you said. After all that's happened, *I owe you.*"

She turned for a second to wipe her nose on her sleeve, and I quickly took the gun out of her hand.

Part Three

The Sounds
of Home

All I can remember is bits and pieces of the rest of that afternoon. Somehow I got Cat upstairs to the living room, and sat her down on a chair. I wasn't sure what to do next, but then there was the sound of sirens and a pit in my stomach as I watched two police cars pull up to the curb. The officers had their guns drawn as they entered Cat's house—it was *so* scary. We had to raise our hands over our heads. They searched us for weapons and read us our rights as we tried to explain what had happened, or rather as I did, since Cat wasn't saying a thing.

Next, I was pushed into the back of the police car. My whole body was shaking. I couldn't stop crying. I remember watching some girl (who couldn't possibly be me) getting handcuffed and told to "Get in." They put Cat in the other car.

As we drove to the police station, I stared out the tinted window, trying to piece together what had happened. The familiar streets of my neighborhood looked surreal—kids innocently riding their bicycles or throwing baseballs to one another in the street, enjoying the late afternoon sun. I remember thinking that I'd never be that carefree again.

It was even worse in the sweltering-hot police station. I was so sure they were going to lock me up, throw me into juvenile detention, and that Alison wouldn't be able to stop them—and what's worse, I believed she might not want to.

Where did they take Cat? I wondered. Did Paige tell the police that I set her up? Did they think I knew what Cat was planning? I was so frightened.

I had to wait in the hallway on the second floor, on a long, uncomfortable wooden bench, which was rock-hard and sticky with sweat. They had removed my handcuffs, but an armed officer was guarding me and two boys who were slouched on the bench with shackles around their feet.

Where was Alison? I knew she was working, but it had been almost two hours since I'd left a message at home and on her cell phone! Was she giving up on me? Trying to teach me a lesson? The detective had offered to let me call somebody else, but I knew Francis had already left for his motorcycle trip. Who else would even care?

When I finally saw Alison hurry off the elevator, I practically flew into her arms. "I'm so sorry! It was completely my fault. Please don't let them send me away!"

"Just tell me what happened," she said nervously. "Don't worry. I'm not leaving here without you." She stepped back for a moment and smoothed my damp hair as her worried eyes searched my face.

"What took you so long?" I asked, sobbing.

"My cell phone died," she explained. "I didn't get your message until I got home. I'm so sorry, you must have been frantic."

I thought she'd be angry, but remarkably her eyes held neither judgment nor blame. And that's when I finally got it. This was what it felt like when somebody *truly* loved you.

As we sat together outside the detective's office, I told her what had happened. Starting with the beginning of the school year, I told her about all the things Paige had done, about Cat's plan for getting back at her, and my part in it—*everything*.

"I just hate myself! Why did I leave them alone? I

knew there was a gun down there."

Alison looked surprised. "But you didn't know Cat was planning to shoot her! *Did you?*"

No. I didn't know. But maybe I should have.

The detective came out to get us a few minutes later. He was a tall black man with a beaklike nose and a receding hairline. He approached Alison first.

"Mrs. Hauser? You're this girl's mother?" he asked, leafing through some papers.

Alison started to say, "No, I'm just the fos—"

But I interrupted. "Yes, she is. She's my *real* mother," I said forcefully.

Despite the terrible circumstances, Alison smiled. And just like that I knew what I wanted to do. Why had I struggled so much with my decision? Why couldn't I have seen it before? Through this entire ordeal, it hadn't even occurred to me to contact my mother in Alaska . . . even for moral support. It was *Alison* who I'd called, and Alison who came here, and Alison who would always choose me.

Like Francis said, *"what's anyone else done for you in the past three years that even comes close?"*

I knew I wouldn't change my mind again.

I was released to Alison's custody several hours later after forensics confirmed that I hadn't tried to shoot anyone—even though my fingerprints were all over the gun. Paige had supported my story (thank God), but of course it wasn't over.

Not for Cat, anyway. It was just beginning.

June 4

From the police station, Cat was brought directly to a psychiatric hospital in Philadelphia. The officers had suspected she was unstable, and after I told them about her waving the gun around and saying she wanted to die, the psychologist wanted her under close observation . . . somewhere safe.

I felt bad about telling on her, after I'd promised I wouldn't, but Alison said I had to. Cat must have had a change of heart also, because in her statement to the police she said that I had *nothing* to do with the incident—except for bringing Paige there—and most important, that I knew *nothing* about the gun.

June first, the court date for my reunification hearing—when I was supposed to go back to my mother—came and went. I was now on probation and had to be reevaluated before any permanent arrangements could be made for me. Now that I'd finally decided to stay with Alison, I hated waiting to make it official.

I was also really worried about Cat, and called her mother this morning. "Do you have a phone number for the hospital?"

Karen said, "Yes, here it is. Cathy was only trying to scare that girl, you know."

"I guess. But why did she pull the trigger? What if somebody had gotten hurt?"

There was quiet on the other end. "People always want to believe the worst about our family," she said bitterly.

I wanted to tell her that maybe there was a reason for that.

I tried to get in touch with Cat like a hundred times.

The phone at the hospital would ring and ring until somebody picked it up or it would be incredibly busy because everyone was trying to use it at once, since the patients weren't allowed to have cell phones.

When I finally got through, Cat said, "I'm making you a paperweight."

"What are you talking about?"

"In group. Art therapy. They want us to make containers out of clay. To hold all of our sadness. But I'm making you a paperweight instead."

I didn't know what to say.

"You can use it when you print out the pages of your novel."

I almost cried. She'd remembered what I'd told her last summer when we first became friends. Cat always had this gift for knowing what was in my heart—and she would hold it out in front of me so I could see it too.

She asked me if I would come visit her, but I wasn't sure if Alison would let me. "Please, Ronnie. Except for my mother, no one will ever come."

June 5

The other sad and disappointing and terrible thing was that my mother relapsed in her apartment, a few days after the incident with Paige. Midge told me this morning that my little brother found her passed out on the couch, turning blue. She had to be rushed to the emergency room: alcohol poisoning. I can't keep that image in my mind very long; it makes me too upset.

Yet a part of me is relieved that I made my decision to stay with Alison before my mother made hers to drink again, because what if I hadn't? What if I had been there watching my brothers? What if I hadn't found her in time? Would I have ended up in foster care again?

Mom is at this new halfway house in Seward, Alaska—for women only, chronic addicts and alcoholics. She'll have to stay there for over a year. The only good thing that came out of it was that she signed the termination papers, giving permission for Alison to adopt me! We set an adoption date for later next month.

The social workers also made her sign away custody of my brothers; they have been placed in foster care. Although I know my mom is in no shape to take care of them, it makes me depressed and really worried to think about them floating from place to place. Midge says that they will be put on the ready-to-adopt list if Mom can't get better this time. Still, I wonder who will they end up with? Will they be safe?

So now another door has closed behind me forever. We will never live as a family again. As sad as that is to think about, one thing I know for sure: Before I came to stay with Alison, my life seemed like it was propelling toward disaster, and now, well . . . maybe I might have a chance.

June 15

Update on Cat: Still in the hospital, but she's been transferred to another unit where I can't visit her even if Alison would let me—only approved visitors, like family, and not even all of them. Her therapists managed to pry out of her what Bud did, and they determined that she needed intensive, long-term treatment.

She called me once, about ten o'clock at night, the

only time I ever heard from her there. "Ronnie, they're saying I can't go back home!"

"Oh, I'm so sorry, Cat," I said, but I was thinking that she's probably better off there than at home.

The therapists notified Children and Youth, and Bud's taken off somewhere. If her mother knows where he is, she isn't saying. I guess there's a warrant out for his arrest. And now her mother has to move because she can't afford to stay in their house, and she has to go to therapy and do a whole bunch of other things to try to get Cat back. She was complaining to Cat, saying things like, *"who do they think they are, insinuating that I'm a bad mother and telling me what to do?"*

Which makes me think, are some people just not meant to be parents?

June 21

Alison, Francis, and I were sitting outside on the patio on a warm summer's afternoon, as Lucky and Checkers chased each other around the backyard. My job was to keep them from ruining the new flower bed Francis had just planted for Alison, which had huge pink peonies falling over, ready to burst. Francis and I laughed as the dogs skidded into each other, barking and play growling.

(Lucky had sure come a long way since Puppy Kindergarten.)

After a few minutes, Francis got up to inspect a row of shrubbery that was half dead from the winter. "You know, Alison, these bushes should be replaced too. What about some holly over here, or a pine tree?"

Alison seemed annoyed. "Another project? We just finished those flowers. Honestly, I don't have the time or money for all of these ideas of yours—"

"But I was offering to do it for you," he said gently.

"You were?" Alison looked embarrassed. "I'm sorry," she said. "I don't deserve you sometimes."

She went in to get us some iced tea and lunch: tuna on English muffins. When she came back outside with a tray, she also brought the mail. Opening the bills, Alison paused at an important-looking letter. "I wonder what this is about?" she said, sliding it from the envelope. "It's from a lawyer's office in town."

The letter said that Cat was being charged with attempted assault . . . with a deadly weapon!

"Oh my God. I can't believe it!" I cried.

"That poor child." Alison gazed at us over the sheet of paper. "They make her sound like a criminal. Don't they realize how troubled she is?"

"Let me see that," said Francis, his eyes scanning the page. "Ronnie's being subpoenaed to testify."

Alison gasped. "What? How did I miss that?"

"It's right here. They want her in court on the fifth of July."

"I've already given a statement to the police," I said. "Do they think I'm lying or something?"

"You're not, are you?" asked Alison nervously.

I shot her a look. "Of course not!"

Still, it was a horrible feeling. I felt hopeless and helpless and scared.

"What if my testimony makes the judge say she's guilty?"

"It might," Francis said ominously. "But you still need to give your version of what happened that day."

"That just isn't fair!" I insisted. "I've let her down so many times before."

Lucky bounded over and put his head on my lap, gazing up at me with his soulful brown eyes. He could always tell when I was upset about something. I ran my fingers through his soft fur. That calmed me down a little.

"This isn't your fault," said Alison, patting my hand.

"Just tell the truth, and we'll pray that it all works out," said Francis.

"Maybe it will," I said, trying to be optimistic.

But as they both raised their eyebrows with worried expressions on their faces, I couldn't help thinking . . . maybe it won't.

July 4

This morning Alison and I went to Liberty's Fourth of July parade, which was something the parents in this town make their kids do for fun. I didn't much feel like doing anything because I was so worried about testifying tomorrow, but Alison wanted me to get out of the house. "You've been hibernating in your room for weeks!"

I had, ever since we heard about Cat's trial. I'd also been wondering about my unused ticket to Alaska, which was still sitting on Alison's desk. I got a sick wave of dread whenever I thought about my brothers being stuck in a strange foster home (who knew how they were being treated?) and I wondered if Alison would ever consider letting me go up there to check on them.

Alison thought the parade would be a good distraction. We had been invited to watch it from her friend's front yard at the corner of Penn Avenue, the main parade route. After breakfast we walked up the street, with Alison carrying a plate of brownies for us to snack on.

"Your friend lives *here*?" I asked, as I followed her onto the plush lawn. Her friend lived right across the street from Paige!

"Oh," Alison said, understanding immediately. "I'm sorry. I didn't think. Do you want to go back home?"

"No. It's okay. I have to face her sometime, I guess." I hadn't seen Paige or any of them since the day of the incident. Alison had let me finish up the two weeks of the school year from home and skip graduation—and none of them had called me.

The parade had already begun. The high school marching band strutted by, followed by a group of little baton twirlers in sequined outfits, red, white, and blue.

Then a whole troop of Boy Scouts lagged behind the procession of antique automobiles, and there was an opening, a big wide space, through which I could easily see Paige and her parents sitting across the street in wicker chairs on the lawn.

Although it was warm outside, and humid, someone had draped a white crocheted shawl around Paige's shoulders. Her hair was limp and she was wearing a striped shirt and an old pair of cutoff jeans. Her face looked drained, like she was recovering from a terrible ordeal . . . and I guess she probably was.

Seeing Paige again made me remember a conversation I'd had with Alison this morning over breakfast. "Whose fault do you think it was?" I asked her. "I mean, could I have possibly stopped all those bad things from happening?"

"It doesn't make sense to blame yourself, Ronnie. Yes, there were some things you could have done differently—but other people made choices too. Even Cat. You can't keep dwelling on it, honey. Try to let it go."

But I *can't* let it go. Last night, I woke up from a terrible nightmare again. I crawled into bed with Alison, soaked in sweat and shaking. When I closed my eyes to fall back to sleep, I could still see Paige crouched on the floor—and Cat with that gun in her hand. I can't stop myself from seeing it.

(Sometimes I'm afraid it will be all I'll ever see.)

I wish I could turn back the clock and start over. If I could, I would have definitely told someone sooner— about *everything*.

As I gazed at her, I wondered—does Paige hate me for bringing her into Cat's basement? Should I cross the street and try to apologize? Will she ever speak to me again?

Suddenly, Paige looked up. She must have felt me staring. It might have been my imagination, but for a brief second, a flash of understanding seemed to pass between us. Something about the choices we'd made, and the chain of events that had unfolded, and how none of us came out of it unchanged.

She smiled sadly, and then slowly looked away, her dark hair hanging in front of her face like a shroud.

I decided maybe that was all the conversation we needed . . . for now.

July 5

The courtroom was foreboding, with its high ceilings and fancy marble walls and rows of pews like in a church. A white-haired judge, a kind-looking woman, sat behind a tall wooden desk. On the wall was an American flag.

The prosecution went first. Francis had warned me that they would try to make Cat look as guilty as possible, but I still needed to tell the truth. It was horrible being called to testify against her, just as I thought it might be, especially with Cat sitting at the front table, with her empty black eyes on the floor. As they swore me in with my hand on the Bible, I knew there was no question about me telling the truth. I just hoped it would be enough to save her.

"Did you ever see the defendant with a gun before the day of the incident?" asked the lawyer. *Oh my God,* how did he know to ask that? He was young and smart and had a blotchy red birthmark on his left cheek.

"Yes, when I slept over at her house."

"Did she say she knew where the bullets were located?"

"It's not loaded. But I know where he hides the bullets."

I looked at Cat. "I guess."

"You guess—or you *know*?" the lawyer snapped, making me feel like a criminal too.

"She said she knew where Bud hid them. But she didn't tell me *where*."

"What about Paige Jamison? Did the defendant ever say she wanted to teach her a lesson?"

I looked at Francis with a pit in my stomach. This was going to be a lot harder than we'd thought.

"Yes."

And on and on it went. Every question I answered made Cat appear more and more guilty; it was like throwing shovelfuls of dirt onto a shallow grave.

When it was time for Cat to take the stand, her hands shook as they swore her in. After she gave her responses, the judge had to ask her to speak up. I hoped she wouldn't fall apart.

The attorney paced back and forth across the courtroom. "Did you load that gun before Miss Jamison got there?"

"No."

"But you admit that you planned to scare her?"

"Yes."

"Were you angry? I understand she'd done some terrible things to you."

"Yes." Cat looked confused. "But I didn't want to hurt her. Not like that."

"What? Speak up! Are you sure?"

Cat hesitated. "Yes, I'm sure."

Next, the lawyer held up a single bullet—and with it, he sealed her fate. He stood next to Cat, with the bullet in his outstretched hand.

"Do you recognize this, Cathy? It was lodged in the wall behind the stairs. It's from the gun that you fired that day. We found your fingerprints on the bullet's casing. If you didn't load the gun, would you care to explain how your fingerprints got there?"

It was shocking! No one said a word.

Cat slumped in her seat and shook her head. She stared at the floor. "I guess I did it. Okay? But I never would have hurt her. I aimed way over her head. It was only to scare her, I swear."

The judge had no other choice but to send her to juvenile detention. She would find out how long her sentence would be at a separate hearing.

Even as I'm writing this, I still can't believe it—it doesn't make sense. It was like seeing a part of Cat that couldn't possibly be there.

Is that what obliteration can do to a person?

July 16

I thought Cat and I might never be in touch again, except maybe if I'd write her a letter someday, and even then I wondered if she would write me back. So when I saw her screen name online, only two weeks later, I just had to scream.

"Oh my God, Alison! Come quick!"

Alison came running up the stairs. "What's the matter? What's wrong?"

"Cat's online! Can I talk to her?"

Alison's lips went straight. She had discussed with me the need to "reevaluate" our friendship, especially after what had happened in court. "You know my feelings on this."

My eyes were glued to the screen. "I know, but—"

Alison put her hand on my shoulder. "She hasn't had any time to be rehabilitated, Ronnie. I don't want you to get sucked into her problems. You have enough of your own things to deal with." She began to walk out the door.

"Please wait! Can't I talk to her for a second? I've let her down so many times! I remember what it's like to be in a strange place without anyone to count on."

With that, Alison relented. "Not too long, okay?"

I couldn't make my fingers type fast enough.

Hearts4u: hey it's me! ☺

purrfect: who?

Hearts4u: Ronnie. i changed my screen name

purrfect: hey

Hearts4u: i can't believe im talking to u!

purrfect: they give us 10 min online if we make our beds and earn all our points for the day

Hearts4u: is it really awful there?

purrfect: some people r nice. others r not. a few kids did some really bad things to get here, but i guess so did i

Hearts4u: i miss u a lot. so does lucky

purrfect: lucky does?

Hearts4u: when i walk him by ur old house sometimes he whines and cries

purrfect: oh

Hearts4u: im so sorry this happened. hang in there ok?

purrfect: k

Hearts4u: Cat? remember i ♡ u

purrfect: you do? thanks. C U next time. GTG my time is up.

July 17

Happy Adoption Day! It's an easy date to remember; the same day as my birthday except in July. It was nice to go into court for something happy for a change. After we signed all the papers, the judge stood in front of the camera with me and Alison and Francis; and even Midge nosed her way into the picture. So now it is official, my name is Veronica Lynn Hauser (still an *H* for my last name, which feels like I'm keeping a tiny part of my past).

Afterward, Francis, Alison, and I sat in Applebee's celebrating—and discussing my upcoming trip to Alaska. After hours of debating the pros and cons, Alison had finally agreed to let me go! The trial and adoption were over, and my mother's counselors at the halfway house thought it might help her recovery if she could see how well I was doing. If it could help her, that would be great, but mostly I wanted to check on my brothers, so they would know somebody cared about them and to make sure they weren't being abused or anything horrible like that. I'd heard about a girl who was missing for over a year in foster care—and nobody even knew she had *died*.

I was excited about the trip, but at the same time it was making me incredibly nervous to think about going. Alison really wanted to come with me, I could tell, but could my mother handle meeting "that Alison woman"? And how would Alison manage being around her? I thought I should go by myself (like that was ever going to happen) but surprisingly, Francis offered to take me. I hadn't even considered that.

Alison seemed upset. "What do you mean, *you'll* take her?" she said to Francis.

"I'm all done with classes," he replied. "I only meant if it would help you out. Weren't you worried about missing more time from work?"

"Not *that* worried," she said. "As her parent, obviously, I should be the one to go." She was looking at him like, *why are you complicating the issue?*

Francis was apologetic. "I'm sorry. I only meant . . . am I interfering?"

"I'm getting used to it," she said, smiling and kissing his cheek.

He shook his head, embarrassed. "Of course, it's up to you to decide."

Alison clasped her hands under her chin. "Then it's settled. I'll go online and see if I can get myself a last-minute deal on a ticket. Isn't it exciting, Ronnie? Just the two of us. A real adventure!"

I began pushing the food around on my plate. "Alison? Please don't be mad, but I would rather it be Francis."

"But why?" she said, looking from him to me like

we'd conspired against her. "I've got an itinerary all plan—"

Francis put a hand over hers. "Please, I think I understand." He turned to me. "Would it be hard to have both of your mothers . . . in the same place?"

"I'm sorry," I answered, nodding. "I think it would be way too uncomfortable—for everyone."

August 1

It was a good decision for Francis to take me, so why was Alison acting so uptight? We were eating breakfast, and she kept jumping up to get another cup of coffee and wiping the counter and asking me if I remembered to pack warm things just in case it was chilly, since the weather changes all the time in Alaska (according to the guidebook, which she'd been studying for days).

"Did you pack a sweater? Your raincoat? Warm socks?"

"What are you so stressed out about? You've been like this all week."

"I know I'm being ridiculous," she said, "but what if you like it there and don't want to come back?"

Was she serious?

"Hello? That's why you adopted me, right? I'm obviously coming back."

"She's still your mother, Ronnie, no matter what else she's done. I understand all too well what that means."

The look in her eyes told me that she might never get over the fear of losing me.

The morning seemed to drag on forever, but I went up to clean and straighten my room, and pretty soon I had finished packing the big suitcase that Alison gave me last Christmas. I was in the bathroom rinsing my tooth-brush when Francis arrived in the car. As soon as I heard the front doorbell, I hurried downstairs, lugging the heavy suitcase behind me.

"I'm ready," I announced. "Let's go."

I was so excited I had butterflies in my stomach. I'd never been on a plane! I couldn't wait to see my little brothers. Alison and I had bought them a few magazines and some toys we hoped they'd like.

"Okay. Do you have your ticket?" Francis patted his jacket pocket to check for his. He gave Alison a long hug good-bye, lifting her up in the air.

Her eyes were glistening as she peered over his shoulder. "You don't have to leave yet, do you? It's going to be awfully quiet around here."

"Oh my God," I cried, "it's only for a week!"

"*Hopefully,*" she answered, smoothing down her skirt.

I rolled my eyes. "Please, not again."

She twisted her hands together and glanced at Francis. "Why did I ever let the two of you talk me into this?"

Francis tried to be patient. "Alison, don't worry. We'll be fine."

Lucky was pawing at my leg, whining for attention. He seemed to know I was going somewhere, but his whining also gave me a good idea.

"Sit, Lucky!" I said, and he listened to me right away.

"Good dog," said Francis, looking impressed.

I tried to make a joke. "Look, Alison. You know I could never leave Lucky. Not permanently, anyway. No offense, but you might forget to walk him. Or feed him. Or by accident leave him out in the snow or rain."

She laughed, like I hoped she would. "That makes me feel better. I have insurance. No matter what happens, Lucky stays here with me."

"Exactly," I said, but I was also secretly excited, thinking she had much more insurance than that: I'd left behind a surprise for her.

Francis took his keys out of his pocket and squeezed her hand. "We really must hurry if we're going to make our plane. I'll call you as soon as we get there."

She touched my hair. "Safe trip. I love you."

I hugged her hard. "Love you, too, *Mom*," I said.

Alison watched us walk out to Francis's car. He carried my suitcase for me, opened the trunk, and put it inside. I slid into the front seat and waved to her from the passenger's side. She looked so sad standing there, but I knew that soon she would find the surprise I left for her and realize all she meant to me.

I tried to imagine the exact moment that she might start missing me and go upstairs to my room to put away my clothes or stare at the posters on my wall, because it was then that she would notice the black plastic bag, my original bag, sitting out on my bed.

That was the best part! My gift to her. This morning I'd cleaned everything out of it and put all my things away. You see, I'd left the empty bag on my bed *on purpose*. And I knew she would completely understand the reason why.

August 2

Fog covered the tops of the mountain peaks that towered over us on either side of the highway. Waterfalls crashed down the mountains in torrents—like huge bucketfuls being dumped over the side of a ship. Francis was driving us to Seward, Alaska. It was about two hours from the airport, directly south of Anchorage.

The peninsula we were traveling around, according to the guidebook, was called Turnagain Arm. And the twisting, turning road we were driving on was called the Seward Highway, which really was the only road from Anchorage to Seward; at least that's what the man at the rental car place had told us.

As we drove along, I got a glimpse of the rugged, rocky coastline, tall pine trees, and the crystal blue sea. The man had told us that there were places you could stop and view whales spouting if you were lucky: minke whales, which are gray whales with a white band on each flipper.

"How about bald eagles?" I asked him, as Francis signed the papers for the car.

"If you look real hard," he said, laughing, "you might."

The first time we saw an eagle, I screamed and made Francis pull over so I could take a picture. It was pecking at a dead animal at the side of the road. This eagle was the biggest bird I'd ever seen, with its signature bright white head. But then as we saw another one a few yards away, and then down the road, five more, we realized why the man had been laughing. Eagles are about as common here as robins back home.

It was stormy at the exit for Seward, with rolling gray clouds and big puddles (more like lakes) on the highway, but some of the clouds had parted close to the top of the mountains, allowing the sun to peek through. The sun sparkled off this huge body of water that Francis said must be Resurrection Bay. I wondered who named it that and why. "See what it says in the guidebook," Francis suggested. But I didn't have time, because I had to help him read the map with the directions to my mother's halfway house—we were almost there.

We drove into the small town, past the center, which had a few restaurants, a bakery, and an Arctic Tacos (there must be a chain!) and farther out, past the railroad, Francis said, was the port where the cruise ships docked. We turned down a side street and there it was: Seward Recovery House.

Francis parked the car in the lot and walked me across a large front porch with rocking chairs, and we rang the bell. They unlocked the door, and buzzed us into the homey-looking building, and Francis told the receptionist I was there to see my mother.

"I'll be okay," I said to him, after I signed in. "Could you please go wait in the car?"

There were lots of windows in the reception area, and the floors were shiny like new. Suddenly, there was my mother coming down the hall, her sneakers almost running the last several steps. She looked so different from what I remembered. I noticed that she was wearing her hair clipped close to her neck now, which made her heart-shaped face look thin, almost gaunt. Her eyes were hollow without the spark of life I'd gotten so used to seeing in Alison's. Even her arms and legs looked thin and bony jutting out of loose shorts and a cotton T-shirt.

"Look at you!" my mother cried.

When she came closer it was obvious that I was now a good few inches taller than she was. She reached over to give me a hug. "You're all grown up!" she said, putting her arms around me awkwardly. As I let her pat my back, I couldn't help thinking: people can grow a lot in three years.

We went into the living room where Mom told me they held group therapy and sat in front of the fireplace. They had a roaring fire going (even though it was summer) because, after all, this was Alaska. As we sat together on those red plaid couches, I didn't know what to say. How can you make up for three years with one conversation?

"So how's school?" she asked. "I mean how did you do this past year?"

I told her about school and Lucky, and then shared a little about Alison and Francis, like how he loved to garden and what a great cook Alison was, but I didn't want to go on and on about how wonderful they were, trying to spare her feelings.

Then she told me about living at the halfway house, and what "step" she was on (in the twelve steps from AA) and how she just knew that my brothers were looking forward to my visit. I had heard from Midge that they were really excited to see me, but I was still worried about how they were adjusting to foster care.

"It'll be good for them," said my mother. "To see family. Especially Derek. Every time I relapse, I think he hates me a little bit more. . . ."

It was funny she should say that. I didn't want to tell her that sometimes I'd hated her too.

"You've gotten so pretty," she said, touching my hair. "Let me go get my camera, okay?"

When she returned, a woman in an ankle-length dress peered into the room. She was talking to another woman with dark skin and hair. "Bettina!" my mom called, waving her over. "This is my daughter! I told you she'd come! We look like sisters, right? Take a picture of us, okay?"

As we waited for them to finish their conversation, my mother whispered to me, "Bettina was addicted to crystal meth. She was sent here all the way from Ohio."

We posed in front of the fireplace: my mom with her arm tightly around my waist, pulling me close. I remembered Alison telling me once that pictures never lie. I wondered if the photograph would capture how uncomfortable I felt standing there.

My mother took the small camera from Bettina and put it into the pocket of her shorts. "When I get them developed," she offered, "I'll send you a copy."

Another woman (a therapist, I guess) came into the room and announced that Group would begin in five minutes. Several residents were already gathering, finding their places on couches and chairs. I was struck by the differences in their appearance: from a middle-aged, overweight lady with a cane to someone a little older than me (with pink hair) who was wearing a long, striped scarf. All so different, but with the same disease.

"I'd visit some more," my mother whispered, "but I can't make the others wait."

Suddenly I felt a lump in my throat. It was going to be sad and somehow final saying good-bye to her; sort of like letting go of a dream. We went down the hallway and through the reception area. She walked me out onto the wide porch with the green painted rocking chairs and a view of the snow-capped mountains looming behind us.

"Well, good luck, Mom. Stay sober, right?"

"You could visit again tomorrow?" she suggested.

"I'd have more time. It's the official visiting day."

"Maybe," I replied, but I think we both knew I wasn't coming back.

She lit up a quick cigarette and the smoke from it drifted over the porch railing. "Ronnie? I want to tell you something. . . ." Her eyes were dark, pleading. "It's like for all these years I've been dead inside."

I shook my head. "I'm not mad at you anymore, if that's what you're asking. I figure some people get trapped into thinking they have no other choices, even when they do."

All of the air seemed to go out of her after I said that.

"So you'll write after I send the picture?" she said, hugging me one more time.

When I didn't answer immediately, she seemed annoyed. "Can't you at least do that for me, Veronica Lynn? Stay in touch?"

I shrugged. "I don't know . . . maybe. I can try."

Before she could ask for anything else, I ran down the stairs.

Francis was standing by the rental car; his gaze fixed on something up in a tree. I smiled when he told me it was another eagle. He gave my mom a wave, but I don't think she saw him. We got into the car as she went back inside.

After I fastened my seat belt, I pulled down the visor and scanned my face in the lighted mirror. "Do you think I look like her?"

He lifted his eyebrow, like when he doesn't know what to say. "Do you want to?"

I hesitated. "Not really."

Francis smiled. "You look like yourself, Ronnie. Perfect. Just like you."

Then he started the car and we pulled out of the muddy parking lot, away from the mountains and the pine trees and the sparkling clear waters of Resurrection Bay. We headed back onto the highway, leaving behind my mother and those other women, who were all so sick and almost dead inside but trying to come back to life.

That night, as I was lying in the motel room's queen-size bed (and Francis was sleeping on the pullout in the living room), I took out the old picture of my mother—the one of her standing in the snow. I studied it one last time. Then I ripped it in half and threw it into the trash can; I wasn't going to need it anymore.

August 6

My brothers' foster parents lived near the University of Alaska, so their place was easy to find—right off the main highway. As we drove up to their condominium, we saw a group of sweaty-looking boys playing basketball in the parking lot. I tried hard to see if one of them might be Derek, but they were too far away to tell for sure. A smaller boy was riding his bike around a pond. He looked so familiar! My stomach was all fluttery—I just had a feeling he could be my little brother.

Francis spotted the number on the door: 116. A man wearing a plaid shirt and very tight jeans answered it when we knocked. His slippers were the light brown color of a fawn. He immediately threw his arms around me. "Oh, there's no mistaking whose sister you are!" he said in a loud, booming voice.

He yelled out to the parking lot, "Derek! Danny! She's here!"

The little boy, Danny(!), pedaled fast on his bike, jumped off, and ran up the sidewalk. He had wavy, light brown hair and scabby knees. Derek was slower leaving the basketball game. He ambled up the walkway, trying to act nonchalant. When they got to the doorstep, my brothers stood there solemnly, not knowing what to do.

"Hey," I said, smiling.

"Hello," said Danny, a shy little five-year-old.

Derek looked down and kicked at a pebble with his shoe.

Their foster dad rubbed at his chin, smiling curiously. "Boys! You've been waiting for her all week! Now give your big sister a hug!"

He sort of pushed all of us kids together. The top of Danny's soft head came just past my waist; he hugged me so tight. But Derek was stiff and held back, so we barely touched.

Francis introduced himself and shook the man's hand. "I'm a good friend of Ronnie's and her adoptive mother. It's so nice to meet you."

"Call me Kip," the man said as he invited us inside. "And this is my partner, Robert."

Midge had warned me to not to be concerned by the fact that two men had custody of my brothers. "They've been screened very carefully," she said.

But I figured as long as they were taking good care of them, who was I to judge? Francis said he completely agreed.

Robert, a very tall man with a bushy beard and longish curly brown hair, got up immediately from where he was working on his computer. "Welcome, welcome. We're so glad you could come all this way!"

After we talked for a few minutes, they invited us into

their small kitchen for lunch. Robert served us lemonade in green bubble glasses while Kip made the sandwiches.

As Derek sat across from me at the round wooden table, I noticed he had our mother's same heart-shaped face and hazel eyes—except that his eyes seemed hard and angry.

"I saw Mom yesterday," I told him, trying to make conversation.

Kip handed us each a sandwich on a white plate, with a pickle on the side.

"So?" Derek peered under the top layer of the sandwich. "What is this? Ham? You know I hate ham!" He flipped the sandwich onto the floor, and as he did he knocked over Francis's glass of lemonade.

"Whoa," said Francis, trying to make a joke. "I didn't see that coming."

Kip glanced nervously at Robert. "Please clean that up, Derek."

"Right now! It spilled on the floor," said Robert, handing him some paper towels.

Francis helped him wipe under the plates. "Ronnie thought their mother seemed to be doing well, considering."

Derek's head was still under the table, but little Danny perked up right away. "Did you hear that I found her? The ambulance man said I saved her life!"

Derek resurfaced with a scowl. "Yeah, so she could sign our butts into the system," he said. "Good job, Danny." He threw the paper towel onto his plate and began to storm away from the table.

"That's enough," said Robert sternly. "Sit down, please. Your brother *should* feel proud of what he did."

Derek sat down again, and the kids were quiet as we

ate our lunch, with Francis and the two men talking about what sights we might visit while we were in Anchorage. Robert taught at the university, so that gave him and Francis something in common. After we finished, Kip suggested that Derek show me his room, while Robert took Danny for a dentist appointment that they couldn't cancel which would only take an hour.

The boys' room was cheerful. Colorful posters of famous basketball players were framed and hung on the closet doors. They had bunk beds with navy blue comforters, and they also had a PlayStation and a small TV next to the door. It was so nice and cozy-looking that I felt better and better about them being here.

"This is really nice," I said, flopping onto the bottom bunk.

"I guess," said Derek. His thumb was already on the controller of his video game.

"Trust me. I've been in plenty of foster homes; this one's not so bad."

Derek spun around and glared. "Are you serious? I frigging hate Mom for doing this to us! Dan is her little baby, so he feels sorry for her—but I never want to see her stupid face again!" He impulsively threw one of the controllers. It made a loud bang as it hit the tin trash can near the door.

We heard quick footsteps coming down the hall. "Everything okay in here?" Kip poked his head in and saw the controller lying by the door.

"Now, son, what did we say about throwing things?" It was like *déjà vu.*

No more throwing things or you're going back.

"I didn't throw it," said Derek defiantly, "it just slipped out of my hand." He stared at me, like, *you're not going to tell, right?*

Kip shook his head. "We just bought that game for you boys two weeks ago. Make sure it doesn't slip out of your hand again." He left the door partway open and went back down the hall.

I suddenly felt worried that Derek might purposely try to ruin their chances of staying here.

"You know, I almost got kicked out of a place for doing something like that. Actually, I did get kicked out of a lot of places, before I finally ended up with Alison."

"So?" Derek picked up the controller as if he were going to begin playing again, but then he paused. "Maybe I want to get kicked out of here."

"You do?"

"I don't know. Sometimes." He shrugged. "They're homos, you know."

I smiled. "Yeah, but they're nice to you, right? You know, Alison, the lady who adopted me? Kip reminds me of her—I mean, you can tell that he really likes you. I was angry too when I first got to her house. I'd been in so many places that I didn't care about anything. I half expected her to send me back, so I stole stuff. I lied. I guess I hurt her pretty bad, but she stuck with me anyway."

Derek's eyes grew wide at what I was telling him. "So?"

"So why don't you just give them a chance?"

The next morning we drove out to Exit Glacier in their car, and we walked out onto the blue-green menthol-colored ice. After that, Robert and Kip took us on a tour of downtown Anchorage. We saw the moss- and flower-covered roof of the log cabin visitors' center and the shops with genuine Alaskan gold-nugget souvenirs.

(I bought a new charm there for Alison.)

They showed us a museum and the University of Alaska, where Robert taught an American history course. But, believe it or not, out of all of the things we saw, what I liked the best was the small bronze statue of the Iditarod sled dog on a street corner in downtown Anchorage, which my brothers insisted on showing me.

"You still like dogs, right, Sis?" said Derek, smiling. Robert had his arm around his neck in a fake choke hold. Derek didn't pull away, but seemed to welcome the physical contact. (I was learning that boys like to rough-play a lot.)

The dog statue was on a pedestal. It was life-sized with a harness on his back. As I rubbed the cool metal of his nose (for good luck), he reminded me of Lucky with his smiling, happy face . . . but also because these dogs have the courage to pull people on long, dark journeys into the light. And as much as I had hoped that my mother would get better, as I rubbed his nose I made a wish that my brothers would find a home with Robert and Kip.

After three days together it was almost unbearable to think about leaving them. Who knew when we'd all be together again? As we lugged our suitcases out to the rental car, I tried to hold back my tears.

"How would you boys like to spend some time in Pennsylvania?" said Francis unexpectedly, as we were saying good-bye.

"What?" I shook my head, totally surprised.

"I checked with Alison last night," he explained. "She suggested maybe over Christmas vacation—or for a few weeks next summer?"

The boys let out a whoop!

Kip nodded. "We can bring them down. I've always wanted to see Gettysburg, and the Liberty Bell."

"Ronnie lives in Liberty," said Danny. "Is the bell close by your house, Sis?"

Derek beamed at me, and so did Francis. We all were grinning from ear to ear.

August 29

It's the end of August now, my absolute favorite month. The air has been warm and heavy since we returned from Alaska and it's scented with the tea roses that Francis planted underneath my bedroom window.

Sometimes, if the breeze is blowing just right, I get a whiff of those roses, and they make me want to cry. Their smell is so honest and sweet (that's one reason), but I think mostly it's because they will always remind me of one of the best days of my life: the afternoon Francis planted them—right after we got back from visiting my brothers, when he and Checkers moved in with us for real.

It may sound strange, but ever since our trip to Alaska, all of the bad things that happened to me seem really far away. Alison says that's because I'm learning how to put the past behind me.

I like to lie in my bed reading or writing just about every night—that's my routine. Sometimes, if it's quiet, I can hear the sound of the holly bush scraping against the side of the house. Other times, if we've had a warm spell, like lately, I can hear the cicadas' rollicking chorus. (Francis says they are complaining about the heat since they don't have air-conditioning and neither do we.)

By the time I turn out my light, there is always the sound of Alison opening the back door and letting the dogs outside one last time. Then she and Francis make sure everything is locked up, and they murmur their late night thoughts to each other on the way up the stairs. Finally they push open my squeaky door to check on me, which is completely unnecessary but nice just the same.

These are the sounds that make up my life now. They are good sounds, comforting sounds. I guess you could call them the sounds of home. But there's one sound I don't think I will ever have to listen for again, a sound that won't haunt my dreams anymore or steal my hope away.

Perhaps you've already guessed what it is.

It's the sound of someone leaving me.

Nationwide, nearly 600,000 children are in foster care. About 40 percent of them are teenagers; half of these are girls.

At any given time there are at least 134,000 children waiting to be adopted.

Organizations that help:

Camp to Belong reunites foster brothers and sisters through camps and other programs. To volunteer, donate, or start a camp in your area, call 303-791-0915 (camptobelong.org).

Child Welfare League of America is committed to engaging people everywhere in promoting the well-being of children, youth, and their families and protecting every child from harm.
(cwla.org) or 202-942-0244.

National Foster Parent Association: 800-557-5238.